BOBBY GOLD

Bobby Gold

Anthony Bourdain

First published in Great Britain in 2002 by
Canongate Crime, an imprint of
Canongate Books Ltd, 14 High Street,
Edinburgh EH1 1TE

10 9 8 7 6 5 4 3 2 1

British Library Cataloguing-in-Publication Data
A catalogue record for this book is available on
request from the British Library

ISBN 1 84195 327 X

Typeset by Palimpsest Book Production Ltd.,
Polmont, Stirlingshire

Printed and bound in Denmark by Nørhaven Paperback A/S

Bobby in Color

Bobby Gold at twenty-one, in a red-and-white Dead Boys T-shirt, blue jeans, high-top Nikes and handcuffs, bending over the hood of the State Police cruiser, arms behind his back, wished he was anywhere but here. The beach would be nice, he thought, as the trooper to his right read him his rights. The beach would be great. Cheek pressed hard against the hot metal of the cruiser's hood, Bobby wondered: if he held his head just right – so that his ear cupped against the blue-and-white car – would he be able to hear the ocean?

The rented Chevrolet Caprice sat on the shoulder, between two cruisers, bathed in flashing red and blue lights. Styx had come on the radio just as they'd pulled him over. He had been happily listening to Monkey Man by the Stones, singing along, in fact, volume all the way up when he'd seen the lights in his rear-view mirror, and in the excitement and confusion of the moment, had neglected to turn the radio off.

Now Styx was playing on the radio, always and forever the sound-track to any future memories of this ugly event. Damn, thought Bobby.

Bobby wondered how the rental company dealt with a situation like this. Would he be charged for the extra days that the car was held for evidence? Who would come and pick it up?

What if the cops tore the car apart? This was a worst case scenario as there were three kilos of cocaine hidden inside the spare tire – and another two kilos behind the seats. Would the guy from Avis take a taxi to the police impound lot, and then drive the car away – or would another employee drive him over, then follow in convoy? As the cops pulled him upright by his hair and walked him over to the rear of one of the cruisers, held his head as they pushed him into the back seat; Bobby found himself curiously detached from events around him.

He would not be sleeping with Lisa tonight – that was for sure. He wouldn't be lying in the bed they shared in the Stimson Dormitory, listening to Brian Eno and sniffing Merck cocaine and smoking hydro. Lisa would not, later, when the quaaludes kicked in, look him in the eyes and turn up the corner of her mouth in a dreamy smile while she sucked his cock. Not tonight. Tonight he was going to jail.

His parents, the already disappointed-in-their-son Dr and Mrs Sherman Goldstein, were not going to be happy about this. The words 'This is the last time—' echoed in Bobby's head as he vaguely remembered some previous outrages he'd committed: the time he'd passed-out in his parents' bed with a check-out clerk from the Pathmark, a fully packed bong still in one hand. The time he'd wrecked their car – sinking it into a water hazard on the green of the local country club. The time he'd been expelled from Horace Mann. The time he'd been expelled from the Englewood School for Boys. The shoplifting misunderstanding . . . He hoped that if his parents – after wailing and bemoaning the miserable fate that brought such a disgrace of a son into the world – couldn't do anything to help him, maybe Eddie could. Eddie could fix anything. He'd been in trouble his whole life – and yet he'd never spent a night in jail. Eddie, Bobby hoped, would know what to do.

Bobby Gold in an orange jumpsuit, handcuffs and leg-irons, shuffled into the courthouse and sat down next to his parents' attorney. Things did not look good. Eddie had not been any help. He wasn't even in court today. Bobby examined the jurors' faces, not liking what he saw.

The old bat at the end; juror number twelve, was shaking her head disapprovingly. She had a daughter in college, Bobby recalled from *voir dire*. She was thinking about all that coke – all that pharmaceutical-grade cocaine, headed in Bobby's car to supply college kids. Might as well have been her daughter's college – to get her daughter hooked, turn her daughter into a coke-sniffing, dangerously underweight coke-whore, tossing off scabby drunks at some imagined truck-stop for her fix. Juror number four didn't look too friendly to Bobby's cause either – a retired jarhead with two sons in the service. With that haircut, he was a definite guilty vote. Things did not look good.

When they gave him ten years, Bobby was not surprised.

Bobby Gold in an orange jumpsuit, stood quietly in line for tuna noodle casserole, coleslaw and lime jello. The other convicts on line in front of him and behind were thick-necked, over-muscled gladiators compared to the scrawny, pencil-necked Bobby. He'd have to exercise – and fast. He'd have to get big, bulk up, get tough. Tomorrow he'd get a tattoo. That would be a start. Something baddass. He had to get big. It was going to take a lot of lime jello.

He was adding muscle. He read the muscle magazines after his cell-mate was done with them. He went to the prison library and read up on anatomy, nerve clusters, bones, pressure points, martial arts. He'd been – supposedly – pre-med in school, so he could order books from outside. He knew what to look for.

Bobby Gold in a towel in the communal shower asked his buddy LT how to get the other convicts off his back. Two cholos from the Mexican gang had tried to jump him earlier in the week, and yesterday, one of the Muslims, a whippet-thin ex-junkie who called himself Andre had taken a parker roll right off of Bobby's tray. What to do?

'You'll have to kill somebody, little brother,' said LT, rinsing the shampoo from his eyes.

'Who?' asked Bobby. 'Who should I kill?'

'Anybody'll do,' said LT.

Bobby Gold on a gurney with squeaky wheels, two knuckles pushed all the way back to his wrist, was hurried to the prison infirmary in restraints.

His nose was broken, ribs cracked, spleen ruptured. There was a three-inch puncture wound below his right shoulder where air whistled from a lung. A chunk of Andre's flesh was still stuck between his molars from when Bobby took a bite out of his cheek. Bobby felt a little bad picking Andre, but he hadn't been big enough yet to tussle with the other convicts. And Andre had asked for it. Bobby was watching 'One Life To Live' in the day-room – and fucking Andre had changed the channel to the fucking Jeffersons. Hadn't even asked if anyone minded. Bobby had looked over at LT and LT had smiled and shrugged.

He didn't think he'd killed the smaller man, though he'd certainly tried everything he could. After Bobby had kicked him in the balls from behind, he'd kneed him in the head, stepped on his neck and then broken both his own hands whaling on Andre's face. When Andre's buddy shanked him from behind with a sharpened toothbrush, he ignored it . . . When Andre grabbed him, he bit him hard until he let go. He kept hitting him until Andre's eye went sideways in its socket and stayed that way. Bobby kept hitting him until the guards came and pulled him off. Just like LT had said he should do.

From now on, thought Bobby, he'd have as many fucking parker rolls as he wanted.

Then he passed out.

Bobby Gold, in a red-and-white Dead Boys T-shirt, blue jeans, and high-top Nikes, stepped through the high electrified fence at the perimeter of the prison. It was February, and he was freezing. He looked around to see if anyone had come to meet him, but there was no one. Lisa hadn't written him, so she sure as hell wasn't coming. His parents had turned their backs on him forever.

Where was Eddie?

BOBBY AT WORK

Bobby Gold, six-foot-four and dripping wet, squeezed past an outgoing delivery of Norwegian salmon and stood motionless, smelling of soggy leather, in the cramped front room of JayBee Seafood Company, taking up space. Men in galoshes, leather weight-belts and insulated vests jockeyed heavily loaded hand-trucks around him. No one asked him to move.

Everybody smoked – their wet cigarettes held in gloved hands with the tips cut down. Men ticked off items on crumpled invoices with pencil stubs, stacked leaking crates of flounder, mussels, cod, squid, and lobster, swept crushed ice into melting piles on the waterlogged wooden floor. At an ancient desk by the front window, a fat man with a pen behind his ear was making conciliatory noises into the phone, blowing smoke.

'Yeah . . . yeah . . . we'll take it back. Yeah . . . I know . . . the dispatcher missed it. Whaddya want me to do? What can I say? I'll send you another piece – no problem. Yeah . . . right away . . . center-cut. I got it. Right . . . right. It's leaving right now.'

When he hung up, the fat man called back to somebody in the rear. 'Send twenny pounds of c.c. sword up to Sullivan's! And bring back what he's got!' Then he looked up, noticed the large figure in the fingertip-length black leather jacket, black pullover, black denim pants and black cowboy boots, obstructing commerce in his loading area.

'Yo! . . . Johnny Cash! Can I help you with something?'

'I come from Eddie,' said Bobby Gold, his voice flat, no expression on his face.

The fat man at the desk rolled his eyes, took a deep hit on a bent Pall Mall and jerked a thumb towards the rear. 'He's in the back office.'

Bobby pushed aside long plastic curtains that kept the cold from escaping a cavernous, refrigerated work area. Salsa music was blaring from a portable radio at one of six, long work-tables where more men in long white coats smeared with fish blood packed seafood into crates and covered it with ice. But the dominant sound here was a relentless droning from the giant compressors that kept the room chilled down to a frosty thirty-eight degrees. They were gutting red snappers around a central floor drain, and there were fish scales everywhere – like snowflakes in the workers' hair, clinging to their knives, on their clothing. Black and purple entrails were being pulled from the fish's underbellies, then tossed carelessly into fifty-five-gallon slop buckets. Against one wall, a triple stacked row of grouper seemed to follow Bobby's progress across the room with clear, shiny eyes, their bodies still twisted with rigor.

Another room: white tile, with a bored-looking old man working a hose while another picked over littleneck clams and packed them into burlap. Bobby's boot crushed a clam shell as he swept through a second set of plastic curtains and into the rear offices. Two bull-necked women with door-knocker sized earrings and bad hair sat talking on phones by a prehistoric safe, a sleeping Rottweiler between them. Bobby opened Jerry Moss's door without knocking and went inside.

'Oh, shit,' said Jerry, a sun-freckled old man, hunched over a pile of price quotes and bills of lading.

'Hi, Jer',' said Bobby, sad already. The old man looked particularly tired and weak today – as if a good wind could blow him over. Bobby noticed with unhappiness the bottle of Maalox on Jerry's crowded desk, the dusty picture frame with Jerry's immediate family clustered around a fireplace, the half-eaten brisket sandwich peeking out from its wax paper wrapping.

'Is it that time again?' said Jerry, feigning surprise.

'I'm afraid so,' said Bobby.

Jerry sat back in his cracked leather swivel chair and sighed, 'So I guess this means I gotta take a beating . . . Is that right, Bobby? I gotta take a beating?'

Bobby just nodded, regretting everything that got him here and everything that was going to happen. He felt as trapped as the old man. It had been like that lately – the feeling bad part. Even with the tough guys, the mouthy, think-they're-smart assholes who he'd straightened up in recent weeks – the big-shouldered power-lifters who'd thought they didn't have to pay because of their hulk-sized chests and their bad attitudes – Bobby no longer took pleasure in proving otherwise. The technical satisfactions of a job well and precisely done just didn't cut it anymore – replaced by a growing sense of . . . shame – a tightening in the stomach.

Jerry Moss was sixty-two years old. He'd had, as Bobby well knew, two heart attacks in the past year, and a recent bypass operation. His last trip to Florida, the old man had come back with a small melanoma on the left cheek which had had to be surgically excised. And he was suffering as well from conjunctivitis, shingles and a spastic colon. He was falling apart by himself.

'How bad does it have to be,' asked Jerry, shifting uncomfortably in his chair.

'It's got to be an arm – at least,' said Bobby, controlling his voice. Any hint of reluctance now would give the old man hope – and there wasn't any. 'That's what he said. An arm. And of course, the face. You know how that is . . . There's gotta be something for show.'

The old man winced and shook his head, studying his desk top. 'That's just fucking great . . . I guess it don't matter I got the money now, does it? I mean . . . shit, Bobby – he knows I'm gonna pay . . .'

'He knows that, Jerry.'

'I mean . . . Bobby . . . Boobie . . . I got the money right here. I can pay now, for fuck's sake. This second. It's right there in the safe.'

'Jerry . . . he doesn't care,' said Bobby, sleepwalking through this part, trying to think about a faraway beach, running an advertising jingle through his head, wanting to get it over with. 'It's not about that and you know it. I'm not here to collect. You're late. That's the point. That he had to ask.'

'An arm . . .' mulled Jerry. 'Shit!' He looked pensively down at his body, as if taking inventory. 'That's just great . . . That's just . . .' He struggled for a word . . . came up with '. . . boffo.'

'What can I say?' said Bobby, shrugging.

'You could say, "Forget it,"' said Jerry, more exasperated than frightened. 'You could say, "What the fuck" and walk away from it . . . That would be a nice fucking thing to say . . .'

'Never happen,' said Bobby. 'Not today.' He lit a cigarette and sat down across from Jerry. He could see the fear starting to come on, welling up visibly now behind the old man's glasses, sweat forming on Jerry's upper lip as the memory of the last time Eddie had had to send him a message began to come back.

That time had been awful, Bobby knew. He'd been on vacation and Eddie had sent two oversized kids from Arthur Avenue to do the job, and predictably, things had gotten out of hand. They'd whaled the shit out of Jerry for fifteen minutes – beaten him within an inch of his life. If memory served, they'd broken both of the old man's legs, his collar-bone, forearm, nose and instep – then smashed his teeth so badly he'd had to have them all replaced. He now wore complete upper and lower plates – they made him whistle slightly when he spoke.

'How many times has it been now, Jerry?' asked Bobby – though he knew the answer. 'I mean . . . Jesus . . .'

'This'll make four,' replied Jerry, almost defiantly, poking his chin out slightly – a bit of business that didn't quite make it as bravado.

'It's pathetic . . . Really. You're not a young man . . . Why the fuck you gotta be such a fucking donkey?'

Jerry just smiled weakly and shrugged his shoulders – looked out the dirt-streaked window at the rain coming down.

'Nobody likes this, Jerry,' said Bobby. 'I certainly don't like it. You think I like this shit? Coming here?'

'Oh yeah?' barked the old man, raising his voice so it cracked slightly. 'Those two retards he sent over the last time? They liked it, Bobby . . . they liked it fine! Those two behemoths? They had a great fucking time, those two . . . I swear to God . . . the one kid? He's dancing on my fucking stomach? Guy's getting a fucking boner!! Oh yeah . . . Those two . . . they was all over me like a bunch a drunken Cossacks. They fucked me up good those two. Real good . . . They were having themselves a real good fucking time busting me up like a day-old fucking biscuit.'

Jerry had gone pale recalling the incident. He tried quickly to buck himself up. 'Hey . . . I should look at the bright side, right? At least he sent you this time. I should be grateful. I should be relieved. Am I right or what?'

'I brought some pills,' said Bobby, reaching into his wet leather jacket, coming out with a bottle of Demerol. 'Take three now. I'll wait . . . I'll wait around for them to kick in, okay? Then it won't hurt so bad . . . That's the best I can do for you, Jerry. The pills . . . they help a lot.' He passed the bottle over to Jerry, watched as the old man tilted his head back and dry-swallowed three. He was used to taking medication.

'Drink?' offered Jerry, motioning to a fifth of Dewars on the dirt-encrusted window sill. 'Since we're gonna be here a while . . .'

'Yeah . . . sure, thanks,' said Bobby. He fetched the bottle, poured two drinks after blowing the dust out of two promotional coffee mugs on Jerry's desk. Bobby's mug read 'JayBee Seafood' with a cartoon drawing of a leaping salmon on the side. Jerry's mug had a picture of a smiling Fred Flintstone on it, and the words, 'Yabadaba-Doo!' in bright red block letters.

'Cheers,' said Jerry. He poured his drink down in one gulp, coughed, then asked for another. Bobby poured.

'Why don't you just pay the man on time,' said Bobby. 'Like you said . . . you got the money. Why piss him off like this – for nothing?'

'Liquidity problems,' explained Jerry, looking at the younger man like he was explaining the bond market to a pool boy or a gardener. He swept his arm through the air. 'Cash flow . . . You know . . . It's ponies and pussy, pussy and ponies,' he said. 'And the dogs. I went the dog track down there at Hialeah? I don't have to tell you what happened,' Jerry smiled weakly. 'That ain't ever gonna change, Bobby . . . so why shit anybody? What? Am I gonna tell you it ain't never gonna happen again? C'mon!'

'If you say so . . .'

'I get to pick the arm?'

'Sure,' said Bobby. 'Your choice. You pick it.'

'I hope I pick better than I pick winners.'

'Yeah . . . no shit.'

'The left. I think. Yeah – the left,' said Jerry. 'I'm a lefty, but—' he lowered his voice, 'I jerk off with my right.'

'Too much information, Jerry. I didn't need to know that.'

'What – I'm too old to jerk off? I need that arm! First things fucking first!'

'Whatever you say.'

'How long . . . how long you think before I can use it again?'

'Three weeks in a cast,' said Bobby, talking about something he knew for sure. 'Four weeks tops. And the new casts they're making these days – they're much more lightweight. You'll be able to get around with it sooner.'

'Fabulous,' said Jerry.

They were both quiet for a while, Bobby sipping his Scotch, gazed idly out the window into JayBee's rear alleyway, listening to the rain pelt the thick panes of alarmed glass and the distant whine from the compressors. The Rottweiler, awake now, poked his head into the room, a filthy squeaky toy between his massive jaws. Seeing no one interested in playing with him, the big dog turned and left, the toy making hiccuping sounds.

'What's the dog's name?' asked Bobby.

'Schtarker.' said Jerry, uninterested. 'That's Yiddish, if you didn't know. People used to say that about you.'

Bobby let that go – consulted his watch.

'Few more minutes and I'll be ready, okay?' said Jerry. 'I'm startin' to feel them pills.'

'No problem,' said Bobby. 'I don't have to be at the club for a while. I've got time.'

'How's that working out for you?'

'Good,' said Bobby. 'It's going good . . . I'm head of security now.'

'Nice for you.'

'Yeah . . . It's okay.'

'You ever get anybody there I'd like? You know . . . somebody . . . somebody I could take Rose to see? She loves Neil Diamond. You ever get Neil Diamond there?'

'No . . .' said Bobby. 'We had . . . let's see . . . we had . . . Lena Horne once . . . we had Vic Damone and Jerry Vale. We had him.'

'Yeah? . . . Good?'

'Yeah . . . they were good. You know . . . Not my kind of music, but good.'

'Bobby . . . If you ever get anybody there . . . you know . . . that Rose would like . . . I'd appreciate it. If you could get us in. She'd love that. If I actually took her out sometime. They got the dinner and the dancing and everything over there, right?'

'Yeah . . . the whole deal. And the food's not bad.'

'Lamb chops? I like a good lamb chop.'

'Yeah . . . we got that.'

'Beautiful!'

'I'll put you on the list anytime you want to bring her,' said Bobby.

'Eddie . . . He ain't gonna mind?'

'As long as you fucking pay on time, Jerry, he won't give a shit. You can do the fucking hokey-pokey on the table – he won't care – he's never there anyway. Just call me when you want to come.'

'Thanks . . . I appreciate that.'

'So,' said Bobby. 'You ready?'

'Shit,' said Jerry, exhaling loudly.

'Take off your glasses, Jer' . . .'

'You gotta do that?'

'Do what?'

'The face . . . You gotta do the face?'

'Jerry . . .'

'I dunno . . . I thought . . . maybe just the arm would be enough . . .'

'Jerry . . .' repeated Bobby, standing up.

'Awright . . . awright . . . Jesus Fuck . . . Lemme get a tissue at least.'

'I brought a handkerchief,' said Bobby, reaching again into his jacket, this time for a neatly folded cotton square. 'Here. Keep it.'

'Always prepared,' muttered Jerry, sourly. He removed his glasses and put them carefully on the desk. 'They teach you that in the Boy Scouts? What did you used to have to say? "A Boy Scout is . . . trustworthy, loyal, helpful, friendly, obedient, cheerful, thrifty, brave, courteous, kind, clean and—"'

Bobby hit him across the nose with the back of his hand. Quickly. It was a sharp, precise blow that knocked Jerry into his chair-back.

'Shit!' said Jerry, honking a red streak onto his shirt front, then covering his face with the handkerchief. He rocked silently in his chair for a moment while Bobby looked around the room for a fat enough book to finish with.

'Get it over with!' hissed Jerry. 'Do it now . . . while I'm distracted!' He rolled up his shirt sleeve.

Bobby found what he was looking for – a thick, hardback copy of *Mollusks and Bivalves of the North Atlantic*, and quickly placed the book in front of Jerry on the desk. Jerry knew the drill. He compliantly laid his thin, blue-veined arm against the spine so that the hand was raised, then closed his eyes. 'Do it!' he said.

When Bobby brought his fist down on Jerry's radial ulna – the thinner of the two bones between wrist and elbow – there was a muffled snap, like a bottle breaking beneath a pillow.

'Ohhh . . .' moaned Jerry, tears squeezing from the corners of his eyes.

'Oh . . . Bobby . . . that hurt . . . it hurts . . .'

'It's over now, Jerry,' said Bobby. He wanted to comfort the old man now – wished he could put his arms around his shoulders – even kiss him on the cheek like he'd had to as a child.

'It hurts,' said Jerry. 'It hurts worse than I remembered.' Bobby went out and found a clean apron on top of a locker. When he got back, Jerry was still rocking back and forth, the injured limb held close to his body, his eyes still closed.

'C'mon, Jerry. Here we go,' said Bobby. He fashioned a serviceable sling out of the apron, helped the old man's arm into it, then primly adjusted it around his neck.

'Motherfuck!!' said Jerry, through clenched teeth. 'It's hot. It feels hot . . . and it hurts . . .'

'Hey . . . It's over,' was all Bobby could think of to say.

'Yeah . . . thanks,' said Jerry. 'Thanks for breaking my arm.' A thin dribble of blood ran from one nostril, collecting on his lip. The whites of his eyes were turning red – as intended. Bobby felt the urge to lean over and blot the nose with a tissue, but resisted.

'It could have been those kids from Arthur Avenue, Jerry,' said Bobby, lamely.

'Yeah . . . you're right. He coulda sent the kids,' said Jerry, bitterly. 'I love this! Like I'm supposed to be grateful? You broke my fucking arm!!'

'What hospital you want to go to? I can drop you at St Vincent's, you want.'

'Fuck you, Bobby. I'll walk over to Roosevelt.'

'St Vincent's is better . . . You won't have so much of a wait, Jerry. It's cleaner. C'mon . . . I'll take you in a cab . . .'

'Get the fuck outta here Bobby, okay?'

'It's raining, Jerry . . .'

'I know it's fucking raining, Bobby Gold . . . Stop it, already . . . You did what you hadda do. Now get the fuck outta here and leave me alone.'

'I'm sorry, Jerry. It's my job. This is what I do . . .'

Jerry looked up at him with sudden and unexpected clarity. 'I know . . .' he said. 'That's what's fucked up about you, Bobby. You are sorry. You got no fucking heart for this shit – but you do it anyway, don't you?' He turned his face away, as if looking at Bobby disgusted him. 'What the fuck happened to you, for fuck's sake? Nice Jewish boy . . . educated . . . and you're beatin' on old men – your uncle . . . your own mother's brother, for a fuckin' living. Some fucking life you got, Bobby . . .' His voice cracked, barely audible. 'Little Bobby Goldstein, all grown up. Your father – he must be very proud . . .'

Bobby flinched. 'Fuck you, Jerry . . . I wouldn't have to do this shit – you paid your debts on time. Don't start talking about family – the way you live – all right?'

'Awright . . . I'm sorry,' said Jerry. 'I'm sorry . . . I shouldn't have said that . . .' He looked out the window, voice steadier now, and sadder. 'Who am I to judge a person?'

It was coming down hard on 9th Avenue when Bobby and Jerry emerged from JayBee Seafood. The old man was looking drugged and dreamy now, his eyes pinned from the Demerol, mouth slack at the corners.

'Let me get you a cab,' offered Bobby for the last time, signalling with his hand.

Jerry waved him away. 'You take it. I'm not fucking helpless here, Bobby. I can take care of myself. I was having guys busted up worse than this when I was half your age – those two guinea cocksuckers he sent the last time? Next week, the very next week – from my hospital bed – I call Eddie and have him send those two down to see some other schmuck owes *me* money – so I ain't gonna curl up and die cause I gotta stand up for another ass-kicking, all right? Now get lost, you little pisher . . . tell that midget gonniff cocksucker you work for he can send somebody over tomorrow to pick up the money. Now leave me alone . . . And say hello to your mother.'

When Bobby left him, standing hatless and coatless in the rain, looking up 9th Avenue towards Roosevelt Hospital, the old man was weeping. Bobby saw him holding the handkerchief to his nose as his cab pulled away from the curb. He watched him through the raindrop patterns of the cab window as Jerry slowly started to walk, one foot in front of the other, shoulders hunched protectively over the broken arm, growing smaller in the distance.

Bobby the Diplomat

Bobby Gold in work clothes; black sport jacket, black button-down dress shirt, skinny black tie, black chinos and comfortable black shoes, pushed open the double doors onto the mezzanine level of NiteKlub. Below, on the dance floor, heads were bobbing in the smoke and the strobes, the heavy bass tones from the half-million dollar sound system vibrating through the concrete. Fifty feet away, on his left, the mezzanine bar was doing big business, stacked three-deep with customers. He saw Del, the mezz security man hurrying towards him.

'Bobby! This is outta control! Have you seen this?'

Bobby looked around, saw, as his eyes adjusted to the light, what was happening.

They were kids. The whole fucking crowd. Not one of the customers clamoring for drinks over the upstairs bar looked to be over seventeen. They were everywhere: chunky girls with teased hair wearing camisoles, skinny boys with baggy jeans and sneakers that glowed in the dark – teenagers, shirtless, dressed-up, dressed-down, in make-up, wearing wigs, sunglasses, drag, full nightclub battle-dress – and they were running wild. In pairs, in packs, eyes lit with X, with booze, with animal tranquilizers, ketamine, Mom's pilfered Valiums, ephedrine, mushrooms and God knows what else. Every one of these little bastards was a potentially ticking time bomb. At the small bar, they signalled noisily for Long Island Iced Teas, Kamikazes, tequila shooters, Lite beers and rum and cokes. Bobby could scarcely believe it.

'You gotta do something about this,' said Del, in despair. 'And look . . .,' he added, 'check this out.' He drew Bobby over to the booths running along the mezzanine wall and yanked back a curtain to reveal a short blonde girl, legs in the air on the middle of a dinner table, her drunken boyfriend in a warm-up jacket grunting over her, his pants down around his ankles. Another boy sat slumped in a chair by her head, unconscious, his mouth open, snoring. The girl looked right up at Bobby with uninflected porcine little eyes. She was chewing gum.

'They're going at it everywhere,' said Del, disgustedly. 'I found two in the air conditioning room before. More in the dry goods area. They're fucking all over the place like little bunnies. Can you believe this shit?'

A young girl in a brassiere and blue jeans hurried past them, fell to her knees and vomited into the base of a potted palm. 'Remind me to never have kids,' said Del.

'You have kids, don't you?' said Bobby, reaching for his radio.

'Yeah . . . well, remind me to not let them grow any more.'

Bobby trotted to the lobby, calling into his radio for Tiny Lopez on the street security detail.

'Tiny! . . . What's your twenty?'

'I ousside, man. Whassup?' said Tiny, a three-hundred-eighty pounder whom Bobby had placed out front for crowd control.

'We're shutting it down. Tell the friskers. I'll let them know at the desk,' said Bobby. He squeezed past a long line of kids who were ascending the main staircase, signalled the downstairs bartenders that something was up, drawing a finger across his throat to give them the sign to stop serving. The lobby was packed. It took him two solid minutes to make it the last few yards to the front desk, where Frank, a silver-haired charity-case pal of Eddie's was stamping hands, standing next to two young promoters in shiny sharkskin suits. Bobby shouted to the security men at the door to close it down, alerted Tiny to what was going on over the radio, and had the two friskers move together to block off access at the choke point.

'Shut the doors,' he said, 'Nobody gets in.'

One of the promoters was in green sharkskin, the other, orange. Green sharkskin looked up. 'What the fuck, man?' he said. 'What are you doing?'

Bobby pushed through the crowd of bodies until he towered over him.

'That's it. Show's over,' he said. 'I'm shutting it down.'

'What?!' exclaimed orange suit.

'You heard me,' said Bobby, struggling to keep his voice under control. 'Frankie,' he said, 'who's been carding these people?'

Frank nodded at the two promoters, neither of whom looked to be of age themselves. 'Eddie said they was in charge of the door. They . . . they said that Eddie said it was okay.'

'What the fuck you think you're doing here?' Bobby demanded of green suit – clearly the alpha male of the two. He saw right away that the kid was going to get up in his face. Orange suit moved closer, shoulders back, trying to look bigger than he was. Bobby outweighed both of them together.

'Whass goin' on?' said orange suit in a whiny voice. 'Why we stopping?'

'You costin' us money, bro',' protested green suit.

Bobby slapped him across the face and he fell against the wall like a stunned trout. He grabbed a fistful of sharkskin with his right hand, and a fistful of sharkskin with his left and dragged the two promoters into the cloakroom where it was a little quieter, pushed them both up against the coat racks.

'What kind of fuckin' jerks am I talkin' to here?' he demanded.

'What the fuck you talkin' about?' said green suit. Orange suit was too shaken to talk.

'Eddie said—'

Bobby slapped him again.

'Let me explain something to you, asshole,' said Bobby, speaking softly.

'This is a business. What do you think's gonna happen – one a these girls you letting in here goes home late, drunk outta her mind, her parents find her puking all over the doorstep with jiz all over her dress?'

'We're straight with Eddie, man. This is our event!' ventured orange suit, finding a little courage.

'Yeah? You know what I think Eddie said?' said Bobby. 'I think he said that you two retards promote the event. That's what I think he said. I think he said that you two do the advertising. That you get the door and we get the bar. That's what I think he said. I don't think he told you two shit stains to let every fifteen-year-old in the five boroughs in the door without carding them. I don't think he asked you twerps to get his liquor license pulled for him!'

'He's gettin' fifteen percent a the door!' howled green suit. 'This is costing us money, bro'!'

'Listen carefully,' said Bobby. 'And watch my hands. Because if I want any more shit outta you, I'm gonna squeeze your fucking head . . . Nobody else is getting in this place until everybody in the club has been carded and checked and all the minors are out of here. You two are half smart? You'll step outside yourselves and make the announcement that everyone is expected to produce valid ID. Not those knock-offs you can buy a few blocks over. We're talking driver's license, passport, photo fucking ID, got it? I'm having my people go through this club to check everyone who's already here. Anyone under twenty-one is out. The sooner we get that done, the sooner we can all go back to making money. Is that understood?'

The two promoters looked at their shoes, humiliated.

'I want to talk to Eddie,' said green suit.

'You want to talk to Eddie?' said Bobby, incredulous. 'Here,' he said, offering green suit his cell phone. 'I'll give you the number. You can call him right now. Interrupt the man's business and explain to him why he's gonna get sued when one of these underage teeny-boppers plows Daddy's Lexus into a bus load a fucking nuns. You want to explain that? Tell him not to worry? That you got it under control? That you definitely ain't gonna put his business in jeopardy, get his license yanked? That he can count on you two to make sure he doesn't wake up tomorrow and see his fucking picture on the cover of the *Post*? . . . Here!' Bobby said, shoving the cell phone under green suit's nose. 'C'mon, tough guy. Call him.'

'Fuck it, man,' said orange suit.

Green suit just glared at him while Bobby continued holding the phone under his nose. When he finally averted his gaze, Bobby turned his back and walked away, giving instructions into the radio.

After calling in additional security from the exits, Bobby put together a flying squad to move about the club, checking ID and escorting those without to the doors. He moved about the club, overseeing the operation – and everywhere he went there was trouble. Outside the Blue Room, he saw his man Nick holding a struggling youth in a full-nelson. Nick had a red welt over his right eye, and was having a hard time controlling the kid without hitting him. A teenage girl was crying on a banquette while her boyfriend was being subdued. A bottle was thrown, and another security man rushed towards the source.

'Little bastard cold-cocked me,' said Nick, through bloody teeth, as he frog-walked the kid down the stairs. 'He must weigh eighty pounds!'

'Get him out,' sighed Bobby. 'And try not to humiliate him in front of his girlfriend. He might come back with a slingshot.'

Another security man, Melvin, with a bad gash over his nose, carried a young man in overalls down the stairs, yelling, 'Coming through!' Furniture was kicked over. More bottles were thrown. Bobby radioed the sound booth and told the head of tech to shut off the music and turn up the house lights.

It took nearly an hour to clear the club. When it was over, only a small group, those who'd actually been twenty-one, huddled by the bar, waiting for it to reopen. Half of Bobby's security team of thirteen able-bodied men and one woman had been scratched, punched, hit with flying objects or in some way injured. Before reopening the bars, Bobby positioned two extra people in the street and doubled the force at the door – in case some of the ejected kids came back with retribution in mind.

When things were finally under control, an older-looking crowd filing into the entrance in orderly fashion – first frisked, then escorted through the metal detectors, then carded, money taken and hands stamped – Bobby looked up to see Frank gesturing worriedly at the door with his chin, pointing out two men who were standing patiently at the head of the VIP line.

One of them was a crew-cut hard case in a turtleneck and trench coat. The other was a fiftyish gent with snow-white hair, thin lips, and flashing brown eyes in a dark suit and camel-hair overcoat. Tommy Victory. Bobby could see the kid in the green suit smirking at him from nearby. Bobby went right over to Tommy, knowing this was trouble, and respectfully offered a hand.

'Tommy. How are you?' he said.

'Bobby,' said Tommy, looking irritated. 'I understand there was a problem here.' He looked around for a second, said, 'Is there someplace we can talk?'

'Yeah, sure,' said Bobby.

He took the two men upstairs and through the Blue Room into the tiny office the banquet department used during the day – and closed the door behind them. Tommy plunked himself down behind the banquet manager's desk without bothering to take off his coat and gestured for Bobby to sit across from him. The big man with the crew cut stayed on his feet, remaining behind and slightly to the right of Bobby, his hand resting ominously on his shoulder.

'My nephew called me a while ago,' said Tommy. 'I'm in the middle of a late supper with some friends . . . and the kid calls me. He says you hit him. Is that true, Bobby?'

Bobby could feel the crew cut's hand tighten on his shoulder.

'Which one's your nephew, Tommy?' Bobby asked.

'Kid inna green suit. He says you smacked him around.'

'If I'd known he was your nephew, Tommy, I would have been a little more diplomatic,' said Bobby. 'I would have called you directly.'

'So what's the problem here, Bobby?' asked Tommy. 'Why you go and have to put a hand on my nephew? What he do? He's a good kid!'

'Tommy . . . They were letting in children. Fourteen, fifteen years old. They coulda got our license yanked. There were teenage girls upstairs getting fucking gangbanged on the dinner tables. It was outta control.'

'So? So you hadda hit the kid?'

The crew cut bodyguard's hand started to move around. Bobby could smell his aftershave.

'Tommy,' said Bobby. 'I'd like very much for us to talk about this like men. Straighten out any misunderstandings. Make amends. Whatever. But, with all due respect to you? If this cocksucker behind me doesn't take his hand offa my shoulder like right now, I'm gonna snap it off at the wrist and shove it up his ass.'

Bobby could feel anger and alarm running like a current through crew cut's hand. He was getting ready to turn around, when Tommy smiled and put up a hand.

'Richie,' he said. 'Give the man some room.' Then he laughed, a long wheezy laugh. 'He'd do it, you know. Bobby here? He's one crazy, bad-ass motherfucker. Am I right, Bobby?'

Richie didn't seem so sure. Though he'd released his grip on Bobby's shoulder, he still loomed close.

'More room,' said Tommy. 'Give him some space to fucking breath. Believe me. You don't want to fuck with this guy. Friends a mine was upstate with this testadura. He's got some sorta kung-fu shit or something. Studied fucking medicine whiles he was up there – like . . . where the bones are and shit. So he knows how to fuck a guy up. He's like a ox, this guy.'

'He don't look like much to me,' said Richie. The first words out of his mouth.

Bobby said nothing, his eyes on Tommy.

'Think?' said Tommy, smiling. 'Tell that to Terry Doyle. You remember Terry? The middleweight champeen? He was up on a rape charge when Bad Bobby was there. Terry liked dark, young, good-looking fellas like Bobby here – and this was before Bobby was big like he is now. Ol' Ter' tried to help Bobby wash his back in the shower one day – him and a bunch a his pals. They say he felt like a fuckin' dishrag when they came for him. Sounded like a bag fulla chicken bones when they loaded what was lefta Terry onto the fuckin' gurney – wasn't no bone over a foot long that wasn't busted. His head looked like a beach ball you let the air outta. You don't want to tangle with this guy, Richie. Just leave it at that. I got confidence we can straighten this out.'

'Thanks, Tommy,' said Bobby.

'I still say you didn't have to smack the kid,' said Tommy. 'That just isn't right. It's disrespectful. A few kids drinkin' . . . gettin' rowdy . . . That's still no reason.'

'One of the kids upstairs,' began Bobby, 'getting poked on the table? I recognized her. It was Christine Failla. She can't be more than fifteen.'

Bobby watched the color drain out of Tommy's face.

'Paulie's kid?'

'The same,' said Bobby.

'Minchia!!' hissed Tommy, screwing up his face in an expression of distaste – and worry. 'Jesus Cheerist!! . . . I was at her first communion for fuck's sake!'

Bobby shrugged and said nothing, content to let Tommy think things through now.

'You sure it was her?'

'Me and Eddie were at her confirmation. Out on the Island.'

'I missed that,' said Tommy. 'I was in AC that week. Jesus . . . Paulie's little girl. You're sure?'

Bobby nodded gravely. 'I saw that, I figured I hadda move fast. What am I gonna do? I can't tell anybody. Your nephew? I don't know who the fuck he is. Even if I did – I mean, Tommy . . . What's Big Paul gonna say? He finds out his baby girl is gettin' porked onna dinner table in Eddie's club? A buncha drunken frat boys watchin' the whole thing? I don't think he'd be too happy.'

Tommy exhaled loudly and actually shuddered. 'You did the right thing, Bobby. You did what you hadda do. Where is that fucking nephew a mine – I'll give him a fuckin' beatin' myself . . .'

Bobby smiled reassuringly. 'Forget it. I cleared the club. Everything's cool.'

'Jesuss . . .' said Tommy. 'Fifteen . . . Listen . . . This goes no further than this room. Nobody . . . and I mean nobody finds out. Paulie hears about this . . . even a hint . . . and I don't even want to think about it. You know, of course – that Eddie's with me?'

'I . . . might have heard something along those lines,' said Bobby.

'Yeah, right,' said Tommy, standing up. 'My nephew doesn't know, right?'

'He doesn't know.'

'Good. He's a sweet kid – but he's got a mouth on him. His mother didn't hit him enough. That's the problem.'

'Kids today,' said Bobby.

'No shit.'

'So we're straight on this?'

'Sure,' said Tommy, making for the door. He stopped and shook Bobby's hand, warmly.

'I'm in your debt.'

Later, Bobby stood in nearly ankle-deep litter on the empty dance floor, watching the bartenders break down and count out. He felt badly about besmirching the reputation of a fifteen-year-old girl who – as far as he knew, was safely tucked into bed with her stuffed toys somewhere out on Long Island – and could well have been all night. In truth, he hadn't seen Chrissie Failla since Eddie had pointed her out, years earlier, waiting for the pony ride at Eddie's kid's birthday party in Westchester. But it had been a necessary lie. Tommy V had put him, and Eddie, in a tough spot. Smack a made guy's nephew and people have to make hard decisions. Appearances have to be kept up. Allegiances affirmed and reaffirmed. Somebody somewhere sits down with a bunch of old men who aren't even close to the situation and then somebody has to get hurt.

Bobby knew how that worked.

And it wasn't going to happen here.

Not this time anyway.

Bobby Eats Out

Bobby Gold in black Armani suit (from a load hijacked out of Kennedy), skinny black tie, black silk shirt and black Oxfords sat on the banquette of 210 Park Grill and looked uncomfortably at Eddie Fish's sourdough dinner roll. Eddie had torn the thing apart but hadn't eaten any; the bits of bread and crust lay scattered on his plate like an autopsied crime victim. When the drinks came, vodka rocks for Bobby, Patron straight up with a side of fresh lime juice for Eddie, Bobby drained his in two gulps, exhausted already.

At thirty-eight years old, Eddie Fish had not once in his life had to wash his own shirt, clean an ashtray, pick up after himself or take public transportation. He was a little man; five-foot-four in heels, and impeccably dressed today: a charcoal gray pinstriped suit from an English tailor, ultra-thin Swiss timepiece, hand-painted silk tie, shirt from Turnbull and Asser, and Italian shoes made from unborn calfskin. His nails were buffed and polished, and his hair, trimmed twice a week by the same man who'd cut his father's, was neat and curiously untouched by gray. Eddie Fish's skin was golden brown, burnished by strong Caribbean sun, and his pores were clean and tight after a morning visit to his dermatologist. He looked pretty much like the man he imagined himself to be: a successful businessman, a nice guy, a democrat and a citizen of the world.

'They love me here,' said Eddie Fish, one arm over his chair back, motioning for a waiter.

'Can't you just pick something and order?' pleaded Bobby, knowing it was hopeless.

'I need a minute,' said Eddie, his eyes darting around inside his head like trapped hamsters.

The waiter arrived and asked if they were ready to order.

'Would you like a few moments to decide?' inquired the waiter politely after Eddie ignored him, his nose buried in the menu.

'No . . . no. Stay,' commanded Eddie.

For Eddie Fish, menus were like the Dead Sea Scrolls, the Rosetta Stone, the Kabbalah and *Finnegan's Wake* all rolled into one impenetrable document. There were hidden messages, secrets that had to be rooted out before it was safe to order. There was, there had to be, Eddie was convinced, some way of getting something better, something extra – the good stuff they weren't telling everybody about. Somebody somewhere was getting something better than what appeared here. Someone richer, taller, with better connections was getting a little extra and Eddie was not going to be denied.

Brow furrowed, the muscles in his jaws working furiously, he scrutinized each item on the menu, each listed ingredient, his eyes moving up and down the columns, then back again.

Bobby had decided on onglet medium-rare thirty seconds after picking up the menu and he looked around the room, killing time, waiting for Eddie. It was mostly women here; long-legged ones with foreign accents and faces pulled tight, a few weedy-looking men who looked like their Moms had dressed them. They were packed in three-deep at the bar, a host hurrying to air-kiss new arrivals. Their waiter, still waiting on Eddie, looked nervously at the rest of his rapidly overflowing station.

'The oysters . . .,' began Eddie. 'Where are they from?'

'Prince Edward Island, sir,' replied the waiter. 'They're excellent.'

'You have any Wellfleet oysters?' inquired Eddie, looking grave. Bobby nearly groaned out loud. Eddie wouldn't have known a Wellfleet oyster if one had climbed up his leg, fastened itself on his dick and announced itself in fluent English. He must have seen them on another menu.

'I'm sorry, sir. No. We don't have them,' said the waiter. 'We only have the Prince Edward Islands.'

'And . . . what kind of sauce do they come with?' asked Eddie. 'I don't want any cocktail sauce . . . that red stuff. I don't want that.'

'They're served with a rice-wine wasabi vinaigrette,' said the waiter.

'Like it says on the fucking menu . . .,' he could have added.

'Uh huh . . .,' said Eddie, processing this last bit of information, wondering no doubt if the waiter was trying to trick him somehow. Wasabi ... Wasabi ... Was that a good thing or a bad thing?

Bobby saw something being resolved. A decision had been made on the oyster question. 'Can you ask the chef to make me some of that sauce with the shallots in it? What do you call that? Mignonette! I want mignonette sauce. It's like ... red ... red wine vinegar and shallots ... and some black pepper. The shallots – you gotta chop 'em up real small. Can you do that?'

'Mignonette.' repeated the waiter, thinking visibly. Which would be worse, thought Bobby: telling Eddie fucking Fish, known gangster associate, that he couldn't have the fucking mignonette with his oysters – or approaching a rampaging prick of a three-star chef in the middle of the lunch rush and telling him to start hunting up some shallots and red wine vinegar?

'I'll have to ask the chef, sir,' said the waiter. 'But I'm pretty sure we can do that for you.'

By the time he started in ordering his entree, Eddie had kept the waiter at his elbow for five full minutes, the rest of the poor man's station shooting daggers at him from their tables. Eddie, oblivious to Bobby's discomfort, began the tortuous process of grafting together elements from different menu items, designing an entree for himself, figuring out the way it should be served, instead of the way everyone else was getting it. Only fools, as Eddie liked to say, settled for less.

'The hanger steak. How is that prepared?'

'With saffron cous-cous, sir,' said the waiter. 'It's pan-seared, then roasted to order and served with a reduction of Côte de Rhone, demi-glace and caramelized whole shallots. It's very good.' The waiter's offer of an opinion doomed that selection. Eddie wasn't having any.

'And the tuna?'

'That's grilled rare . . . served with roasted fingerling potatoes, braised fennel . . . and a citrus herb reduction,' said the waiter, the first hint of frustration creeping into his voice. It made no impression on Eddie. The poor bastard could hop up and down holding his crotch, get down on one knee and bark like a dog – it wouldn't make any difference to Eddie, who seemed to slip into some kind of a fugue-state when ordering from a menu.

'Okay . . . Okay . . .' pondered Eddie. 'How about . . . let me . . . get . . . the . . . the monkfish. The saddle of monkfish.'

'One monkfish,' repeated the waiter, gratefully, the clouds beginning to part, one foot already pointed towards the kitchen.

'But . . . let me have that with . . . with the sauce from the hanger steak,' said Eddie. 'And like . . . the roasted finger potatoes. That sounds good . . . And what came with the tuna? What was the vegetable with that?'

'Uh . . . braised fennel,' stammered the waiter. Bobby saw the light go out in his eyes. He got it now. He understood, finally, what was happening. Eddie was never letting him go. All hope was gone. This vicious, malevolent little creep wasn't going to be happy until his whole station was up in arms, until his other customers were so pissed off they tipped ten percent, until the chef was pushed to the point of murder. Chefs blame waiters for the sins of their customers, the waiter was probably thinking – and his chef, when he saw Eddie Fish's order, was going to unscrew his head and relieve himself down his neck.

'Forget the monkfish,' said Eddie, changing tack, 'Let me have the turbot instead. Yeah. I'll have the turbot. It's fresh?'

'Yes.'

'Then I'll have the turbot. Grilled . . . with the balsamic reduction and baby bok choy from this pork dish here . . .'

'Yes, sir,' said the waiter, picturing his imminent dismemberment in the kitchen.

'Wait!' commanded Eddie, as the waiter began to turn away. 'Before you bring the fish . . . could you lemme have a Caesar salad?'

'I'm sorry, sir,' said the waiter. 'We don't have—'

Eddie was not deterred. He'd expected this. 'It's simple. You tell the chef, take some egg yolks . . . and some garlic. Fresh garlic . . . and some anchovies . . .'

It went on like this . . . and on. It always did. Bobby had known Eddie since college. Nearly twenty years – and every meal was like this. When the order was, at long last, finally taken, the waiter dispatched to the kitchen to meet his fate, Eddie was still looking at the menu, unsatisfied. He'd study it for a few more minutes, to see, Bobby thought, where he might have gone wrong, doing an after-action report in his head, analyzing where he might have missed something. By now, Bobby had completely lost his appetite. The customers at the tables around them glared, murmuring in French. Bobby, easily the largest man in the room, felt like a circus bear, staked in place, trapped and uncomfortable.

Eddie straightened his tie and put down his menu.

'Isn't this place great? You can't get reservations here. Six month wait.'

'You murder these waiters,' said Bobby.

'Are you kidding me? They love me here!' said Eddie, shooting his cuffs, then rubbing his hands together in anticipation of his oysters and his Caesar. 'You know how much I tip when I come here?'

Yeah, thought Bobby. Twelve percent.

Knowing the back-of-the-house of the restaurant business as he did, Bobby could well imagine how much they loved Eddie Fish here. They probably had a nickname for him. Catching sight of Eddie, moving brusquely across the dining room to his favorite table (without waiting to be seated), they probably said, 'Oh, shit! Here comes that malignant little shit! Please, God . . . Not my station! Not my station . . .' Or, 'Here comes the Pomeranian. Look out! That cocksucker can keep his twelve percent. You take that table. I'm NOT waiting on that fuck.'

What the chef thought of the troublesome Mr Fish, Bobby could only imagine. Considering what havoc he played with the man's scrupulously thought out menu, Bobby would be surprised if there wasn't some small way in which the chef revenged himself. If he hadn't already hocked a big, fat phlegm-ball into one of Eddie's from-scratch Caesars, he was clearly a man of Herculean endurance.

Bobby recalled overhearing one of the NiteKlub cooks, talking about what one could do to a particularly hated customer's food.

'Copper oxide, dude,' the cook had said. 'You can get it in, like, hobby shops, for chemistry sets. You sprinkle that shit in somebody's food, bro'? They gonna slam shut like a book – then it's lift-off time! We're talking projectile vomiting! We're talking explosive diarrhea – that motherfucker's going off like a fucking bottle rocket!'

'What's so funny?' said Eddie, noticing Bobby smiling serenely. His oysters had arrived, and he speared one with a fork, ran it around in his mignonette.

'Nothing,' said Bobby, startled out of his reverie. 'I was just thinking.'

'Oh yeah? . . . Well, think about this: I got something for you to do tonight.'

'What?'

'A tune-up. You gotta go out to Queens and see a guy.'

'I work at the club tonight.'

'Yeah? Well, get somebody to cover for you. This guy needs a talking-to right away.'

'Shit, Eddie . . . You don't have anybody else? I'm over this shit. I don't want to do it anymore.'

'I don't have anybody big enough. This guy is a fucking gorilla. You should see him. He looks like a fucking building with feet. And tattoos. You never seen so many. I think this goof's been in jail.'

'What he do, Eddie? He doesn't sound like a customer.'

'He's not. I brought the Jag in to be fixed – this guy,' said Eddie, pushing away his plate of oysters, only half of them eaten. 'He was supposed to put in a new carburetor. New, Bobby. New. My regular guy comes back from vacation, takes a look under there, says it's a reconditioned piece a equipment. Fucking guy ripped me off.'

'So? Call him up. Tell him what a dangerous man you are. Tell him to put a new fucking carburetor in for Chrissakes . . . What's the problem?'

'This guy doesn't listen to reason. We had a few words on the phone. I make a few suggestions. He tells me to go get fucked. He's a real hard-on this guy. A tough guy. A Nazi. No shit!'

'A Nazi?'

'He has, like, swastikas all over his neck – on his arms. I saw this character when I brought the car in, I couldn't believe it.'

'Why you going to Nazi fucking mechanics, Eddie?'

'He came recommended. What? I don't care for the guy's politics. I don't give a fuck he's got Yasser Arafat, John Tesh, Willie Nelson tattooed on his fucking face – he was cheap. And this other guy said he was good. It's a fuckin' chop shop he runs out there. Tommy V's crew brings him some cars now and again. You know . . .'

'Great. I gotta go all the way out to Queens. Get into it with some fucking hero from AB—'

'AB?'

'Aryan Brotherhood, Eddie. It's a jail thing. Guy's flashing swastikas all over his body, he's probably AB.'

'Oh . . . Then you probably know the fucking guy. It'll be like old home week. Go break his kneecaps and reminisce about the good old days. I can't have this asshole getting over on me, Bobby. It's bad for business. People talk, you know? Tommy's people hear this fucking animal talking about how he pulled one over on me – where does it end? Next thing you know, I'm taking it up the ass from every deadbeat fuck in town.'

'Peachy. And it's gotta be tonight?'

'Tonight, Bobby. It's gotta be tonight.'

Their entrées arrived, but Bobby's appetite was long gone. He picked at his hanger steak, transfixed by the way Eddie chewed with his mouth open.

'Remember in school?' said Eddie, apropos of nothing, spraying food as he talked. 'You weighed, what? One-fifty? One-sixty? I could have taken you! ... Remember we were going to take off Kenny – the guy with the Merck coke? You wouldn't do it. You said he was too big. Remember?'

'Yeah,' said Bobby. 'I remember.'

'That worked out. Jesus, we make money on that or what? I musta put like a six-to-one cut on that shit ... That worked out okay.'

'Okay?' said Bobby, snarling. 'Okay? I got pinched with that shit! I did eight fucking years for that shit! I did your fucking time! Maybe you remember that part?'

'Oh, yeah,' said Eddie, wiping his mouth with the end of a napkin. 'I forgot.'

Lenny's Auto Parts was located in Long Island City, on a deserted street lined with warehouses and fish wholesalers. Lenny's was at the very end, by the Long Island rail tracks; a big, unruly yard heaped with compacted and uncompacted cars, mountains of rusting fenders, windshields, chassis and tire rims, just barely contained by a corrugated steel fence. Next to the house; a garage with graffiti-covered steel shutters. A dog barked somewhere when Bobby got out of his taxi. The light on the second floor was the only sign of life on the block, a single window situated over a dark office space, approached by a rickety outside staircase which wound around what looked like it was once a two-family house.

A Harley was parked out front, on a small square of untended lawn, the grass littered with candy wrappers and beer bottles. Bobby clumped up the stairs, not bothering to be quiet, and banged twice on the door.

The man who answered was enormous, a scowling, fat bastard with redwood-sized arms, a tangled beard with what looked like bits of potato chips caught in it, and the dense mural of tattoos, both professionally and self-applied, which said, 'prison prison and more prison.'

The knocking had clearly awakened the big man. As soon as he opened the inner screen door, his eyes still focussing, the words, 'What is it?' coming out of his mouth, Bobby hit him with a short, chopping right straight into his windpipe. As he staggered back, Bobby crouched down, feet planted, and as the big, hairy beast struggled for his first gasp of air, gave him a roundhouse wallop to the temple. He fell flat on his back with a tremendous crash and didn't move.

'Whatchoo do to my brother?' came a voice from the back of the room. Bobby looked to his right, across a shabby, communal living space littered with beer cans and take-out containers. Sitting in a clapped-out reclining chair, sipping beer from a tall-boy, was an even larger man – also bearded, also heavily tattooed. Worse, Bobby recognized him.

'Bad Bobby!' said the man. 'Dude! You really fucked my little brother up. Guess he'll be out for a while.'

'Lenny?' said Bobby, flustered.

'Yeah,' said the man in the chair, scratching an iron cross over his thorax. 'When you knew me I didn't go by that name. That's Frank there on the floor. He's gonna be pissed when he wakes up. Got a temper, that boy.'

Bobby noticed with dismay the twelve-guage Ithaca shotgun leaning against the side of the chair. Fortunately, Lenny seemed to be making no attempt to reach for it.

'LT . . . LT, right?' said Bobby.

'Right.'

'I'll be dipped in shit!'

'Come on in. Siddown, have a beer.'

Bobby crossed the room, stepping over the crushed cans, the styrofoam containers. A TV flickered silently in the corner, two chubby lesbians going at it on a shag rug on the screen.

'So,' said Lenny, when Bobby was sitting down on a rickety lawn chair by a beer-can-covered card table. 'You got business with little brother? Or you got business with me?'

Bobby thought he heard snoring, looked over against the right wall and saw a black woman sleeping on a bare mattress. She looked pregnant.

'My old lady.' said Lenny. 'I got a kid too. In the next room. He's got the asthma. Got him hooked up to one a those machines. Try not to wake him.'

'I guess I got business with you,' said Bobby, grabbing a warm beer from a half-emptied six-pack on the card table. 'LT. I can't believe it . . .'

'Bad Bobby comes calling. After all this time . . . Who woulda thought.

'Made nice work of little brother too. You look good. You keeping in shape.'

Bobby just shrugged. He was uncomfortable with the situation. LT had been the head of the Aryan Brotherhood at Greenhaven when Bobby had been up there. He'd taken the then gangly and dangerously unprotected young Bobby under his wing, assigning other gang members to look after him. They'd become buddies, playing chess in the day room, exercising together in the yard, talking about history – particularly military history – the fact that LT was essentially a Nazi, and Bobby a Jew, adding a certain playful nature to their relationship.

'So, what's the problem? And who do I got a problem with?' said Lenny.

'Eddie Fish has a problem,' said Bobby. 'Something about a carburetor you sold him.'

Lenny threw his head back and started to wheeze with laughter, his whole body shaking.

'THAT asshole? You comin' all the way out here – the middle of the fuckin' night – chop down my bro' like a freakin' tree – over a fuckin' carburetor? Oh, Bobby. I thought things was gonna be different for you when you got out. We all thought you was gonna go back to school. End up a lawyer or somethin'. Aww, Jesuss. I'm sorry to hear this.'

'I'm not too thrilled with how things worked out either,' said Bobby, his ears burning. Pity from a 350-pound white supremacist car thief did not go down well.

'Let me clue you in, here, Bobby. That little shit comes out here with that fuckin' Jag a his. Says he wants a deal on a new carb. I says I got a new carb right in the back. Cocksucker doesn't want to pay for it. You know who I am? He says. You know who I'm with? Now lissen, Bobby, you know me. I don't give a fuck who he's with ... I'm with some people too – and when they come by my shop? They talk nice to me. I ain't nobody's nigger, right, Bobby? So shithead tells me how much he wants to pay – which is not much. I couldn't get a used carb out of a fuckin' Ford for what he's offerin'. So I tell the kid I got to clout me one out of this nice XJ I happen to know about. Thing's a year old. Practically new. I gave it to the guy at fuckin' cost. This kid I got working for me? He's used to taking cars, Bobby. To order. The whole fuckin' car. Not rootin' around under the fuckin' hood like some kid who's just waitin' to get grabbed. I made a couple a calls to some people and asked about this Eddie fuckin' Fish that's supposed to be such a big shot? And you know what they told me? "Fuck him." Do what you can. But don't bend over backwards, you know what I mean? I did the right thing.' Lenny took a long draught of beer and shook his head. 'What are you doing hanging around with that fuck, Bobby? From what I hear? He's gonna get fuckin' clipped any day now. The people he thinks he's such friends with? They ain't such good friends.' He took another long slug from the can and stared at Bobby while he finished his thought. 'Not like us.'

On the floor, Lenny's little brother stirred. Holding his throat, he raised up on one elbow and stared at Lenny and Bobby sitting amiably together. 'What the fuck?' he rasped.

'Be cool, bro',' said Lenny, his voice betraying no concern. 'You just stay where you is – right there.'

'Fuck that!' said not-so-little brother, managing to clamber onto all fours. 'I'm gonna—'

'You ain't gonna do nothin', Frankie,' said Lenny. 'Unless you want me to get outta this chair and give you the biggest ass-whuppin' a your life. You wake the kid and I'm gonna be real mad at you, little bro' . . . Real mad.'

'Listen, Bobby,' said Lenny. 'As you can see, things are gettin' a little tense and all around here. Tell you what. Tomorrow? You tell that little Christ-killer you work for to come round with his fuckin' Jag. Me and little brother put a nice shiny new one in for him, no charge. Cause it's you? I'm happy to do it. But after that, I don't want to see him no more. Next time he comes around here? There might be some folks waitin' for him. Guy's a fuckin' insect. I don't care what he tells you. The people who count? He's nothin' with them. Only reason he's still alive is some folks figure he ain't worth killin'. Whether you want to tell him that is up to you, bro'. But you know me. I tell it straight.'

'Thanks, LT,' said Bobby. 'I really appreciate it. You were always good to me. Never understood why . . . But you were always good to me.'

Lenny smiled and leaned back in his chair, his eyes narrowing to slits. 'You ain't a white man, Bobby Gold. That's for sure. But you almost white. And we white men gotta stick together.'

'What about her?' said Bobby, indicating the sleeping black woman on the mattress.

'Oh, that?' said Lenny. 'That's love, Bobby. That's a whole different thing.'

Bobby nodded as he stood up to go.

'Listen,' said Lenny, helpfully. 'You better put moron over there to sleep for a while on your way out. He's gonna be all hot and bothered and I don't want him waking the kid or causing a ruckus, he goes followin' you out to the street. Better he sleeps for a while.'

'What?' said Frank, trying to scramble to his feet as Bobby approached him on the way to the door.

'Sorry, Frank,' said Bobby. He side-kicked him behind the ear as he passed by, doing it with his toe rather than the heel. The impact pushed him onto his face. He stayed down.

'Thanks, LT,' said Bobby.

'Be good, Bad Bobby . . .'

'I'm tryin',' said Bobby.

Bobby in Love

Someone was snoring, Nikki opened her eyes, instantly aware of a jumbo-sized, king-hell hangover, her mouth tasting of tequila – afraid to look.

There was a used condom in the ashtray on her nightstand. Nice touch, she thought, pain boring into her skull like a dull drill-bit. Just perfect. She raised herself onto one elbow, feeling nauseated, pushed some long, brown hair out of her face, and examined the hand that was resting limply on her bare hip. Seeing the thick, diagonal callous at the base of the man's index finger, her heart sank. Whoever he was, he was in the business. This was bad. Everybody would know. All the other NiteKlub cooks; the chef, the sous-chef, even the floor staff – they'd all know about it by tonight.

Nikki knew how these things went in the small, incestuous subculture of cooks and kitchens: first, the initial report, then the reviews, then additional commentary. Word would spread. Kitchen phones would be ringing all across town. 'Did you hear who the sauté bitch went home with last night?'

Who had she taken home anyway?

Nikki turned over, carefully, so as not to wake the sleeping man. She held her breath, then pulled down the covers to take a look. It was Jimmy Sears.

'Oh, NO!' she yelped, sitting bolt upright now. She delivered a sharp blow to Jimmy's well-muscled shoulder.

'Get up!! . . . Wake up you asshole!! . . . Oh, shit . . . oh, FUCK!!'

'Morning,' said Jimmy, sleepily, already looking much too pleased with himself. He rolled over onto his back, a morning hard-on poking out from under the sheets, rubbed his eyes and stretched. She considered braining him with the lamp. That would keep his mouth shut. Maybe she could even dispose of the body – bit by bit – if she had her knife kit. She could break him down like a side of veal. How hard could that be? She knew veal, beef, lamb, venison, chicken, rabbit, pork . . . how different could human anatomy be? But her knives were at the club, rolled up in their leather case and safely stashed in her locker – and who was she kidding anyway? This was awful. Of all the rotten people in the world to get drunk with, take home, let between her legs – this had to be the worst-case scenario.

Jimmy, while cute – and hung like a donkey – was the sleaziest, most loud-mouthed Lothario in the restaurant universe: a braggart, misogynist, prevaricator and all-around bullshit-artist. To make matters worse, he was the NiteKlub chef's arch-rival. This wasn't just an embarrassment. This was treason.

Nikki flashed back to when she'd worked for Jimmy – how she'd heard him, on countless occasions, bragging to his entire crew how he'd bagged some round-heeled hostess or rebounding bar customer – the excrutiatingly clinical details: the way Jimmy would imitate the noises a girl had made when he'd 'walked her around the room like a wheelbarrow,' how she'd 'looked like a glazed donut' when he'd blown his load all over her face. The room seemed to tip sideways for a second, and Nikki ran for the bathroom.

She made it to the bowl with no time to spare, hurled yellowish bile into the porcelain, seeing stars. She was in there a long time, intermittently lying naked on the cold tile floor, and crawling back to the toilet, her stomach muscles convulsing with the effort of trying to squeeze out what was no longer there. After ten minutes or so, staring up at the ceiling, the sink making drip drip sounds, she tried listening for Jimmy in the bedroom, hoping he was gone. She thought she heard the refrigerator door closing.

Memory was returning. She recalled Siberia, last night . . . the crowd at the bar, people jammed around the jukebox, Tracy, the owner, dancing with a pastry chick from the Hilton, remembered herself on the couch in the back room, drunk on tequila shots, Jimmy's tongue down her throat – and her with her fingers down the front of his pants, teasing the head of his oversized dong.

'Please kill me now,' she said to the bathroom ceiling, 'I'm ready . . . I deserve to die. Please . . . just get it over with . . .'

When she finally stood up, her vagina hurt. She was horrified by what she saw in the mirror: eyes, mascara-smudged sinkholes, the skin around them puffy and almost bruised-looking from throwing up. Her hair was a rat's nest, sticking out at all angles like it had been teased with a weed-whacker. There were purple marks on her outer thighs where Jimmy, no doubt, had held her while he'd drilled away with his legendary wonder-penis. She couldn't really remember the sex yet – but then Jimmy would be happy to remind her.

She swallowed three aspirin, fighting to keep them down while she ran the water, waiting for the room to fill with steam before she stepped into the shower. She was in there a long time, trying to boil Jimmy Sears out of her pores. When she was done, she brushed her teeth twice, combed out her hair, wrapped herself chin-to-ankles in a long, terrycloth robe, and finally, stepped warily back into the bedroom.

Jimmy, still naked, had made breakfast: two perfectly fluffy yellow omelettes sat plated on the kitchenette counter – a spoonful of pilfered beluga on each one. Jimmy's signature garnish: two antennae-like chive sticks projected up from each mound of pearly grey fish eggs.

'I was saving that caviar,' said Nikki.

'I didn't use it all,' said Jimmy, pouring champagne.

'Where'd you get the champagne?'

'I ran out to the corner.'

'You got dressed . . . ran to the corner . . . bought champagne, came back . . . and took your clothes off again?' said Nikki, horrified.

'Hey . . . It's a special occasion.'

This was enough for Nikki. 'You're not staying. And I'm not eating.'

She avoided looking straight at Jimmy. For all his faults, he had a good body. All the surfing, skiing, in-line skating, handball, golf and tennis (when he should have been in his fucking kitchen) had made Jimmy tan and cut, his stomach ribbed with muscle. Even at 39, he had a boyish, almost irresistibly ingratiating smile that seemed to invite conspiracy and bad behavior . . . He was, thought Nikki, watching him reposition an omelette so that the knife and fork faced her, sort of charming.

He had to go. Now.

'Get dressed and get out, Jimmy,' she said. 'You can take breakfast to go. Take it home to your wife, or your girlfriend or whoever it is these days you're lying to. Just leave.' She sat down on the bed, dizzy again, a sudden stabbing pain in her groin. 'Jesus . . . what did you fuck me with? A pineapple?'

Jimmy shook his head, smiling like a little boy who'd just successfully lifted a comic book, and sat down next to her. He brushed his lips against her shoulders. She shook him off.

'Just leave, please.'

He began to dress. J. Crew polo shirt, khaki pants, Gap blazer, Cole Hahn loafers (no socks of course), a baseball cap with the name of a band on it. God, thought Nikki – how could I have fucked this asshole?

'Whatever you say,' said Jimmy, fully expecting, it appeared, that she would change her mind.

'I say.' said Nikki. Dressed, at least, Jimmy was easier to despise. She looked at the floor, noted with displeasure the trail of clothes she'd worn last night – evidence of her stupidity – a reconstruction of events possible from the shoes kicked into opposite corners, the pantyhose hanging over the rocking chair. The brassiere must have come off last – it peeked out from under a pillow. She didn't see her dress.

'You're losing your hair,' she said.

'I am not!' protested Jimmy. 'Bullshit!'

'In the back. You're losing your hair. You're going bald.'

'I am not going bald!' insisted Jimmy, zipping up his pants but not going anywhere until this issue was resolved. 'I use stuff . . . and it's working!'

'It's not working,' said Nikki, tossing him a loafer. 'Maybe you should get that spray. The skull-paint? Maybe that'll work . . . But the Rogaine? The minoxadyl or whatever it is? It's not taking. Believe me.'

'You can be a mean bitch, Nikki.'

'Yeah?' said Nikki, lip curling as she moved in close. She was taller than Jimmy by three or four inches – and face to face she looked down into his eyes. 'You think you seen mean? Lemme tell you this then, chef . . . I hear one word about this from anybody . . . ever . . . One fucking word about last night – and I'm gonna tell every cook, every waitress, every chef, dishwasher, bartender and busboy in town that yes – I did take you home and fuck you – that I got you drunk, took you home and fucked you. And I'm gonna say that you cry "Mommy" when you come. I'm gonna say that you came in about two seconds, cried for your Momma, wet the bed in your sleep . . . and left a big tuft of hair on my pillow when you got up in the morning. Now get the fuck out of my apartment, you bald fuck. I gotta go throw up again.'

'Are you saying you didn't have a good time?'

'Truth be told, Jimmy? I can't remember one way or the other . . . But I'm sure you were spectacular. Feel better? Now get out.'

Jimmy walked to the door and stepped out into the hallway,

shaking his head. Nikki slammed the door after him. She heard him on the other side, saying under his breath, 'Cunt!'

'Got that right, asshole,' said Nikki. She began dressing for work

Bobby Gold, in black jeans, black, short-sleeved T-shirt and black trainers walked up the steps of the empty club. On the second floor mezzanine, he heard a toilet flush, waited for whoever it was to emerge. The mezzanine was still a mess from the night before – the maintenance crew still busy waxing the dance floor. The door opened and a girl came out, dressed in chef's whites. Bobby had seen her before in the kitchen – they called her the 'sauté bitch' in there, he seemed to recall.

'Hi,' she said.

'Hi,' said Bobby, a little flustered. He didn't spend much time with women – and he was thrown by how good she looked in the sexless, double-breasted uniform and checked polyester pants. 'You're in early aren't you?'

'Yeah,' she said. 'Prep for the party tonight. I gotta get the stocks going.'

'Oh,' said Bobby. She was tall – maybe five-ten, with long, dark hair that smelled like it had just been washed and her eyes – dark, almost Asian-looking pools – flashed with intelligence. There was the hint of a smile – the slightly sour, self-deprecating smirk of someone who's had their ass kicked and survived the experience.

'You a fan of classic comedy?' she asked, seemingly apropos of nothing.

'What do you mean?' Bobby asked, 'Like what? The Marx Brothers? Fields? Chaplin?'

'I meant more like Lenny Bruce,' said the girl. 'Remember him?'

'I saw the movie – if that's what you mean. Dustin Hoffman played him, right?'

'Yep,' said the girl.

'Good movie.'

'Yeah . . . well . . . I don't know how to tell you this – but there's a guy doing a really good Lenny Bruce imitation in one of the stalls in there,' she said, jerking her head in the direction of the bathroom.

Bobby thought no way she meant what he thought she meant. He hurried into the bathroom, walked quickly down to the last stall – the only one still closed, and leaned against the door. It wouldn't open. When he pushed, it felt as if someone had piled a stack of flour sacks against the other side.

He entered the next stall, stood on top of the toilet and peeked down over the divider.

She was right about the Lenny Bruce thing. There was a man in there – pants down around his ankles, one sleeve rolled up, a syringe hanging out of his arm, just below a tightened belt. He was dead, and he was blue, slumped over to one side with his legs jammed against the stall door, eyes staring straight up at Bobby like a lifeless flounder's.

Bobby got back down from the toilet and went back outside. The girl was smoking, sitting on a banquette, watching for his reaction. She'd gone in there, he realized, found the body, and calmly sat down for a piss, before exiting.

'See what I mean?' she said, smiling.

'It's Lenny all over,' said Bobby, unable to take his eyes off of her. He was in love.

Bobby gets Jilted

Bobby Gold in black Levis, black trainers, and black T-shirt, the word 'SECURITY' printed in white letters across the chest, pushed open the swinging kitchen doors and stepped into the noise and heat. He hesitated momentarily by the door, fully aware that this place – of all the various rooms, areas, offices and fiefdoms in NiteKlub – was not his territory. Here he was an outsider, an interloper, completely unaware of the local language and customs. Dinner was winding down – all the entrees were out, only the *garde manger* chef still plating a few forlorn desserts – and the cooks were breaking down their stations, wrapping up *mise-en-place* in clean metal bains and crocks and wiping down their areas. Out in the main dining room, the waiters were beginning to strip the tables, hauling and rolling them off the dance floor. When the last few dinner customers put down their dessert forks and called for their checks, the THUMP,

THUMP, THUMP of bass tones would come rumbling through the kitchen walls, then the smell of chocolate from the smoke machine – sucked in by the powerful range hoods. The Intellabeam system would wink on, bouncing filament-thin rays of colored laser beams off tiny dancing mirrors controlled by computer and joystick in the sound and tech booth. There was maybe a half-hour before the front doors were opened and the lines of people, already two deep and wrapping around the corner onto 8th Avenue, were let in. Two hours from now, every foot of floor space in the main room, mezzanine, Blue Room – even the entranceways, stairs and bathrooms – would be jammed with people.

Bobby stood near the door, unsure why he was even here. He'd told himself, climbing the back service stairs, that he was hungry, that he'd stop by the kitchen to see if there was any staff gruel left over. But that was something he'd never done before. The truth was, he'd come to see the girl. The cook, the one they called Nikki – to look at her if possible, to get close enough, maybe, to smell her hair – just for a second, to look in those eyes, the ones that hurt when they looked at you. He had no plan – unusual for Bobby, who planned just about everything these days – and that made him nervous and uncomfortable. He certainly wasn't going to ask her out, as he'd long ago forgotten how to do such things, and the whole thought was ridiculous anyway.

He hadn't had a woman for years.

From where he stood, awkwardly trying to figure out what to do, he could see Eric, the sous-chef, counting out dinner dupes by the printer, spiking the little slips of paper onto a spindle, his hair plastered to his skull with sweat. A shorter cook (he thought they called him Lenny) was scraping down the grill with a wire brush, bobbing his head along with the speed metal on the radio, bitching in kitchen patois about some violation of protocol that Bobby didn't understand.

'You want truffle jiz? Get your own truffle jiz, cabron. I tired a you raiding my motherfuckin' meez everytime I turn around, *pinchay culero*. Every time you go in the shit, you sticking your hands in my fucking bains.'

Next to him, an Ecuadorian pasta cook named Manuel smiled serenely, shook his head and apologized. Insincerely.

'I sorry my friend,' he giggled, turning towards Eric, who had clearly heard all this before. 'Chuletita no like I touch the station. He like I touch the pinga. *Si! Verdad!* Touch his pinga is okay. Culo, no problem. He like that. But no touch the station.' He reached over and swatted a dirty side-towel at the back of Lenny's head, before dropping down to his knees to mop out his low-boy refrigerators. Two cooks, Segundo and Eduardo, were dumping a tray of indifferently roasted chicken legs into a hotel pan on the pass. Billy, the skinny white boy with the pierced tongue on the *garde manger* station, listlessly tossed salad in a large stainless-steel bowl with his hands.

In the corner behind the line, Nikki was heaving a stack of dirty saucepots and sauté pans into a cardboard-lined milk crate, a cigarette hanging from the corner of her mouth, her chef coat unbuttoned. Bobby saw the pink and red burn marks – like tribal markings – on her forearms, and thought they were the sexiest thing he'd ever seen. Her hair was popping out of its pony tail, long strands falling over her face, and Bobby could not help but be fascinated by how the muscles on her arms swelled and jumped as she slung, one-armed, one heavy load of pans after another loudly into the crate. She hadn't seen Bobby yet. As she leaned over the stove, to remove the burner covers, he stared at the way the boxy, checked poly pants stretched over her ass.

'I'm hungry!' complained Joe, the head tech, with a hoarse, froggy voice. Billy, who relied on Joe for cocaine now and again when the busboys and bar-backs didn't come through (Bobby knew this from observing Joe's mid-shift runs around the corner to the The Full Moon Saloon – and the ensuing not-very-discreet sequence of hand-offs and bathroom visits which inevitably followed) was all too willing to make something special for his patron. No chicken leg and wilted salad for Joe.

In the noise and clatter of the kitchen, Nikki still hadn't seen Bobby, who continued to stand there as if invisible, ignored by the cooks and their protégés from the floor. Unlike Frank, now tucking into a porterhouse steak on a broken chair in the corner, Bobby did not share the impounded guns and drugs from the door with the kitchen crew. He didn't let the cook's friends in for free – or give them drink tickets. No one had dared ask him. Everyone eating something other than the staff gruel in the kitchen at this moment had some kind of special arrangement with one cook or another. The waitress, Tina, was a vegetarian. The usually surly cooks had fixed her up with some grilled vegetables and cous-cous. Because she was cute. Because she flirted with the cooks. Because once or twice a year, after a few drinks, she took Eric, the sous-chef, into the liquor cage and sucked his dick. She sat on the ice cream freezer while she ate; a few powerless busboys and newbies poking unenthusiastically at their chicken legs nearby as they slunk off to eat in locker rooms, stairwells and hallways. Even Hector, the night porter, was being taken care of. He was eating a thick slice of pork loin with sauce and mashed potatoes, probably a payback for giving the kitchen a regular cut of all the pilfered goodie bags from NiteKlub industry parties and fashion shows. He also, apparently, threw them the occasional oddity or archeological find he'd come across when clearing out banquettes, or exploring the sub-cellars the club shared with the hotel nextdoor. There was a covert cooks' lounge, Bobby knew, located in a disused storage closet on the fourth floor, which Hector had furnished nearly single-handedly with stolen hotel furniture, pilfered carpet remnants, even a jury-rigged phone line, so the cooks could call their dealers.

A runner arrived with a tray of cocktails for the kitchen: a large pitcher of Long Island Iced Tea, a pitcher of beer, a few Stoli grapefruits for the Chef – who was now hidden away back in his office, no doubt packing his nose with the new hostess. As soon as he'd dispensed drinks and returned from the Chef's office, two steak frites appeared, (one for the runner and one for the cooperating bartender) as if by magic on the slide, and the runner wordlessly scooped them up and headed for the door.

Bobby, who'd forgotten to eat since yesterday's breakfast, approached the tray of chicken legs.

'Don't eat that shit,' said Nikki, who'd apparently been aware of him for some time. 'I'll make you something.'

Bobby, surprised, stood upright, stammered, as suddenly all the cooks were staring at him.

'Uh . . . sure. Thanks . . . Th-that'd be nice.'

'What?' said Eric, glaring at Nikki through the pass. 'Did I hear right?'

'I said I'd make him something,' said Nikki. 'You got a problem with that? Or does he have to suck you off first?'

Tina, on the ice cream freezer, blushed slightly and the other cooks laughed.

'Whatever,' said Eric, backing down. He looked at Bobby, a sustained stare for a few seconds, then went back to counting his dupes. Lenny, the grill cook, however, kept staring, a look of unrestrained hostility fixed on the new intruder.

'It's not necessary, anything special . . .' said Bobby, not wanting to get in the middle of some arcane tribal political situation. 'I can have this. I can have the chicken.'

'No way,' said Nicole, pushing wet hair out of her face. 'No way you eat that mung. I make you something nice . . . Fish okay?'

'Yeah. Great,' said Bobby, no longer thinking about food at all, really. Trying not to look at the pale expanse of bare flesh between Nikki's sports bra and check pants underneath the open jacket. It looked smooth and hard.

'Ricky!' Nikki barked, calling over a runner. 'Get him a chair and a set-up!'

The runner dragged over a chair from the nearby wall phone, disappeared for a minute and came rushing back with a rolled up napkin and silver. Bobby sat down at the end of a long steel worktable in the center of the kitchen, feeling all the cooks' eyes on him.

'You want something to drink? We got beer, Iced Teas – anything else you want. Just ask Ricky,' said Nikki from behind the line.

'Water. Water is good,' said Bobby, uncomfortable with all the furtive looks and barely concealed scrutiny.

'Ricky!' she yelled, again. 'Bring him una boteilla de Pellegrino! Rapidemente!'

Richard, the Chef, poked his head in the kitchen, a clot of white powder hanging from one nostril, a snap undone on his check pants. 'Eric! How many?'

'About three hundred,' said Eric, not looking up, the last dupe just hitting the spike.

'Smooth?'

'Like Lenny's ass. Like a well-greased machine. We didn't get weeded at all.'

'Returns?'

'Just the one. A refire steak.'

The Chef grunted and went back to his office and whatever he had been doing.

Though there were at least twelve felonies, or violations of club policy, in evidence at this precise moment, Bobby didn't care. He watched Nikki prepare his dinner, absolutely transfixed by her smooth, economical movements behind the line. She seasoned a thick slab of monkfish, grinding black pepper from a mill, then rubbed it with sea salt. She fired up the stove and noisily slapped a pan on it, waiting for it to get hot. Without looking, one hand darted out, grabbed a wine bottle with a speed pourer, and drizzled a little olive oil into the pan, stood back a few seconds, waiting for it to get hot, then laid the fish in the pan with a sizzle and gave it a shake.

Twirling, she fired up another burner, reached for a small saucepot and positioned it over low flame. Bobby saw butter go, a little oil, some shallots. He was amazed how quickly her hands moved, how effortlessly she seemed to handle her knife, chopping the shallots into uniform small dice before scooping them into the saucepot. When Lenny saw her pouring hard pellets of arborio rice into the pan, stirring it with a wooden spoon, he looked shocked. She nudged him out of the way and reached into his lowboy.

'Hey, bitch,' he protested, 'Don't fuck with my meez!!'

'Shut the fuck up, bitch,' said Nicole. 'I need stock. Gimme some . . . And some porcinis. Some porcinis would be nice.'

'Fuck, man . . . they all the way in the back,' complained Lenny.

'Suck my dick,' said Nikki, ignoring him. 'I need stock. I need porcinis. And haul me out some truffles while you're in there, cupcakes.' She gave Lenny's fat ass a gentle pat as he ducked into the low reach-in refrigerator to get her what she wanted.

She laid out a few crayfish tails from her own stores, a bottle of white truffle oil, turned to stir the rice, poured in a little stock when Lenny finally managed to extract some from his crowded refrigerator, stirred the risotto with the wooden spoon. Judging the fish ready to turn, she flipped it with a pair of tongs, put the whole pan in the oven and casually kicked the oven door closed with the side of a food-encrusted clog.

'Damn!' said Lenny, seemingly appalled. 'You making the man truffle risotto?'

Nikki just turned wordlessly back to her cutting-board, reached down once again into Lenny's box to retrieve some arugula, turned, stirred the risotto again, added a little more stock and stirred again – then lowered the heat, looking satisfied, lost, seemingly in thought. Bobby saw she was chewing her lower lip.

'How do you like your fish?' she asked Bobby.

'Uh . . . I don't know . . . Whatever . . .' said Bobby. Noticing that she seemed to shake her head slightly at this, he corrected himself. 'Okay . . . uh . . . medium rare.' This seemed to please her.

'Good. You didn't look like a well-done.' As she turned back to the stove to once again give the risotto a stir, she said 'Good' again, softly this time.

In went the crayfish tails, the mushrooms, and the truffle peelings. She reached down into the oven, a side towel protecting her hand, and removed the fish. In a small saucepan, Bobby watched as she heated a little sauce from a cooling crock a few stations down, whisked in a little knob of whole butter, lowered the flame. Pulling the risotto off the stove, she folded in some arugula, then carefully piled a neat mound in the center of a plate, spun back to the stove and gingerly transferred the fish from pan to plate, resting it at an angle atop the risotto. When the sauce seemed reduced to her liking, she drizzled some around the plate with a large spoon, then stepped back to examine her work, head tilted, seemingly unsatisfied with something. She reached for a bottle of truffle oil over Lenny's station, reconsidered, and then, looking both ways, quickly dodged back into Lenny's lowboy and removed a single, fresh white truffle from inside a moist towel. She was shaving a few paper thin slices over the plate with a small grater when Eric looked up from his cocktail and his stack of dinner dupes.

'White truffle!? White fucking truffles you're giving the guy?' he spluttered, speaking as if Bobby weren't sitting right there. 'Fresh fucking white fucking truffles? Why don't you just yank down his fucking pants? Give him a nice sloppy fucking blow job?'

'I'm thinking about it,' said Nikki, squaring off, giving him a hard, confrontational look.

Bobby turned crimson. Ordinarily, in such circumstances – not that there had been any circumstances like this in recent memory – his first instinct would have been to stand up, walk over to this Eric guy, and squeeze his carotid for him, maybe lift him up off the ground by his throat, give him a few smacks, a few pointed words. But this wasn't about him at all. Nobody was watching him. All the cooks were paying attention to a contest of wills between Nikki and the sous-chef, anxious to see how things were going to turn out. There was something else going on here, too, Bobby saw. All kinds of history – beyond a simple struggle for control. The other cooks looked worried, protective, defensive; Lenny and Billy actually moved closer to the lone woman behind the line, defending her – but at the same time puzzled, and somehow . . . hurt.

Eric threw down the stack of dupes with a look of disgust and a 'Fuck it,' and stalked back to the locker area.

'This okay?' said Nikki, bringing Bobby his meal.

'It looks . . . wonderful,' said Bobby. 'I hope I didn't get you in trouble.' He was trying to get the blow job comment, and Nikki's response, out of his mind.

'Fuck him.'

Bobby took a bite of fish with his fork. 'It's amazing,' he said.

Nikki hopped up onto the stainless-steel worktable and watched him as he chewed, a look of almost clinical detachment on her face. After he took another bite, she leaned forward, reached over and tore off a little piece with her fingers, popped it in her mouth and tasted, pleased with herself. Leaning forward the way she was, Bobby got a good look straight down the valley between her breasts, every tiny bead of sweat coming suddenly, vividly, into focus, Bobby wanting suddenly and in the most terrible way, to lick them off. Instead, he took a bite of fish, a little risotto. It truly was delicious.

'Really, really good. Thanks. So much,' he said, trying desperately not to stare at her tits anymore, focussing intently on her eyes.

'Bon appétit,' she said, hopping down off the table and removing her apron. She crumpled the food-smeared cotton/poly object into a tight ball and hurled it casually across the kitchen, where it dropped neatly – all air – into a laundry bin. 'Three points,' she muttered.

The other cooks were melting away one by one. Bobby and Nikki were almost alone in the large kitchen, when, looking like she was getting ready to leave, she turned back to him and asked, 'What are you doing later?'

Flustered, Bobby found himself saying that he was working – which was patently obvious.

'Until three,' he finally managed to say.

'You got a girlfriend or something?'

'Uh. No,' said Bobby, no phrase book available for this conversation. Totally at sea.

'So. You want to meet me later for a drink?' she asked. Just like that.

Bobby hadn't had a 'date' since before prison. 'After work?' he asked, feeling terribly tongue tied. 'I uh . . . okay. Sure. That would be nice.'

There. He'd said it.

'Sooo . . . I'll go home. Shower all this fish jiz off, change – and I'll see you back here at three . . . Meet you out front.' With that she turned her back and was gone.

*   *   *

She had a drink at the mezz bar on the way out. The bartender there never denied her anything. She'd fucked him in the dry goods area at the last Christmas party – an experience she was unlikely to repeat. His cock, she remembered dimly, leaned noticeably to the left. And he'd smelled of patchouli. The glass in her hand suddenly empty, she had another one, as she felt, strangely enough, nervous about her imminent meeting with the mostly silent and (they said in the kitchen) dangerous Bobby Gold.

'You know what that guy does?' Lenny had said in the locker room, his voice lowered to an insistent whisper. 'He's like a bone man! He busts people up for Eddie Fish! He's a fucking gangster, Nick! I heard that he maybe even kills people!' Lenny had been waiting for her in there when she arrived to peel off her soggy, reeking whites.

'Bullshit,' said Eric, unseen on the other side of a row of graffiti covered lockers.

'He's a fucking faggot. What's with the all-black clothes? Who does he think he is? He's all talk. Another punchy-ass doorman been sprinkling steroids on his fucking Froot Loops. Probably got balls the size a cashews.'

Nikki, in her underwear, peeked around the corner. Eric was cutting a few lines of coke on the lid of a plastic fish tub, a shaker glass of Long Island Iced Tea sitting on the floor next to him.

'Think so?' she said. 'I'll let you know.'

'I'm tellin' you, man. He's into some serious shit,' said Lenny. 'I know . . . I heard from reliable sources. He's been to prison – for like a long time. For murder or some shit.'

'Bullshit,' said Eric, unwilling to believe anything so interesting about the quiet security man who his number-one line cook was clearly planning on fucking. 'All those muscle guys are faggots,' he sneered. 'They all take it in the twins.'

Seeing that Eric was too drunk to talk to – and not caring what he said anyway – Nikki struggled into her jeans, pullover and leather jacket, slung her knife roll over her shoulder and prepared to leave. Lenny looked stricken.

'It'll be fine,' she told the chubby little line cook, pinching his cheek. 'I'm just having a drink with him.'

She left him in the locker room looking dejected, shaking his head.

They all wanted to get in her pants. That was the problem.

Back at the mezz bar – another drink. This one the last. She was worried. All the tall, thin women around her, with their carefully applied make-up, their club clothes. Nikki caught sight of herself in the mirror above the bar and didn't like what she saw, an outcast, a line cook, a guy with a cunt. She watched herself drain yet another drink, looking like nothing more than the kitchen slut – stringy brown hair, a pullover shirt from the fish company, baggy jeans and sneakers. The scent of smoked salmon still lingered on her fingers.

'What the fuck am I doing?' she asked herself, more than once, as she walked somewhat unsteadily over to her 11th Avenue apartment. She hauled herself up four flights of narrow stairs, the hallway smelling of cabbage and boiled corned beef, unlocked her door, and after peeling off her clothes, poured herself another drink and headed for the shower.

Bobby Gold at three-thirty in the morning. Standing outside NiteKlub. Feeling bad.

Nikki woke up fully dressed, sunlight blinding her.

'I can't believe it!!' she wailed, her eyes filling.

Her shoes were still on. A black Danskin top, tiny black leather skirt. 'I can't believe it! I can't fucking believe it!! I am such an . . . asshole!'

The bed was barely disturbed. She'd come home last night, best as she could reconstruct it, showered, washed her hair, done her fucking nails (toenails too, she noticed). She'd brushed. She'd combed. She'd dressed. Jesus fucking Christ – she'd even waxed! Eau de toilette . . . lipstick . . . mascara – even rolled a joint for her three o'clock meeting with the moody security chief. Then she'd rested her head on her pillow for, what? . . . One fucking second? And promptly fallen asleep.

She'd jilted him. The tall, morose Bobby Gold would have been disappointed. She knew that. She could tell he could be hurt. Something about the way he wore his hair long, the way his long forelocks hung down over his face, concealing his feelings.

'Shit!!' she rasped, kicking her best knock-me-down-and-fuck-me shoes onto the floor petulantly, wondering how long he'd waited. Standing there in the dark and the cold outside NiteKlub.

Story of my life, she thought. More questions to which she'd never know the answer. Another road not travelled. Another missed chance. Now she'd never look inside, past those dead shark eyes, past that look – of resignation, acceptance – she'd never know what the other thing was in there, that thing she'd seen for a second or two outside the bathroom that day, the whatever it was that she'd glimpsed somewhere at the sea bottom.

If she'd gotten him in the sack, she'd have known. Another vain, body-worshipping jerk, in love with his own reflection? She didn't think so. He wasn't a cook. There wouldn't have been the bluster, the cynicism. The false bravado, the endless talk about dick dick dick. No smell of garlic and seafood, no corn starch caked under his balls – none of that towel-snapping, jock-like, locker room mindset that Nikki now lived and breathed, it felt sometimes, with every pore and atom.

For the first time in six months, she thought, I put on a skirt. Do my nails. Wax my fucking pussy – and then I pass out.

She wriggled out of her clothes and lay face down on the bed for a while. She had to be at work in three hours. In three hours, she'd have to put on those scratchy poly-blend kitchen whites again, the damp, food-spattered clogs, she'd pick up her knife roll and walk down the long flight of steps to the kitchen and the noise and the boys who loved her but would never understand her . . . the endless, relentless flow of incoming orders, the soul destroying . . . stupidity of it all.

What would Bobby say when he saw her again? What would she say?

She had to get out of this someday. She needed a plan. She thought, for the first time, about what Lenny had been talking about a few days ago in the walk-in. His latest, knuckleheaded get-rich-quick scheme. For a few seconds, Nikki pictured herself on a Caribbean beach, in a bathing suit. A tall umbrella drink in her hand. No burn marks on her wrists. Where would she live in such a place? And with whom? She couldn't picture a house. Or a person.

When she found she was wearing earrings, she hurled them against the wall and started crying again.

Then she did something she'd never done even once in her entire career.

She picked up the phone and called in sick.

Bobby gets Blue

Bobby Gold, in a blue funk, sat slouched back deep in the stained couch, one leg slung over a torn armrest, drinking vodka. Timmy Moon, behind the stick, washed glasses and hummed along to Junior Walker on the jukebox, ignoring the sole customer at the bar – a fastidiously dressed old man in an ancient suit, currently snoring into a puddle of beer. There were two gum-ball machines in the corner, leased, Bobby knew, from Metro Vending – Eddie's company. A joker-poker machine blipped and clicked and beeped against the far wall under the chain-link-fenced piece of glass that had once been a picture window. No one had been able to see through the grime-encrusted square for decades. The poker machine, occupied at this moment by a pencil-necked building super named George, was also Eddie's (Magic Carpet Entertainment Inc.) as was the cigarette machine near Bobby, and the condom machine in the bathroom. Bobby had once joked with Eddie about the condom machine, pointing out that 'no one at Timmy's has had an erection for years.' The beer in the taps was from a distributor associated with Tommy Victory (dba Zenith Distributors), and the vodka Bobby was drinking – what was it – his sixth, seventh? – was from Xanadu Beverage Inc. – also Eddie's – in partnership with Tommy, of course.

Timmy, now lighting another Parliament from the end of its predecessor, did the occasional work for Tommy V – as he had for Tommy's father before him. Part of a long and glorious tradition of murder-for-hire going back three generations of Moons. Timmy's son, James, Bobby had recently heard, had been arrested for menacing and possession of handgun. Bobby remembered seeing James, only a few years earlier, hanging out with his friends on the corner, skateboards and baggy pants and new, white sneakers, wool caps pulled down low over their eyes, in conscious emulation of Latino prison gangs Bobby knew only too well.

The music changed to U2, a development as predictable as the over-aerated Guinness in Timmy's taps, or the wet mass of toilet paper clogging Timmy's toilets, or the inescapable outcome of an evening spent drinking at Timmy's: a hangover, a nose clogged with undissolved mannitol, and unexplained cuts and bruises. The place smelled of vomit and Lysol, something one got used to after a while, and the sweat of the old men who drank up their social security checks there in the afternoons. It was nighttime now, late night, the high-end crowd. Soon, the place would be crowded with bartenders and waiters and cooks, come over after last-call had been announced at more legitimate establishments.

Bobby was punishing himself. He was feeling bad – angry that he'd allowed his hopes to rise, something he'd been very careful not to do since being upstate. This was the price, he thought glumly, of allowing yourself to believe in other people. This is what happens.

All day and into the evening, he'd tried, really tried, not to look in the kitchen – or anywhere in the direction of the kitchen. He'd convinced himself he wasn't hovering by the door at four o'clock when Nikki was scheduled to come in – and he'd pretended to himself that he neither cared nor wondered when she hadn't shown up for her shift. There'd been a short stab of pain every time the door opened and it wasn't her. And when it was clear that she wasn't coming it only made things worse, because now, not only was he wondering why she'd led him on and then not shown up as promised, but where she coud be right now – and what she might be doing.

He felt sick. And the vodka wasn't making things better. Bobby lay his head back on the couch and stared up at the painted-over tin ceiling, Sam Cooke on the box now, angry, angry about how all this had snuck up on him unasked for.

Two hairy bastards in leather jackets and work boots came into the bar holding a car radio, slapped it on the bar in front of Timmy and demanded to know how much he'd pay for it.

'Not interested, gentlemen,' said Timmy, not inquiring if the two would care for a drink.

'How 'bout you, buddy? You want a radio? It's a Blaupunkt. Get fifty bucks for it. Sell it to you for twenny, my man.'

'Fuck off,' said Bobby, not bothering to even look.

'What you say to me?' said the larger of the two – a bearded asshole with a much broken nose and dried blood caked under one eye.

'He tole you to fuck off,' said the other one.

'Get the fuck outta my bar,' said Timmy, holding a cut-down 10-gauge now, what was left of the barrel resting on the bar. A few inches away the sleeping man continued to snore, undisturbed, such was the relaxed, even melifluous tone of Timmy's request.

'What's the matter with you?' said Timmy after the two had left. 'Why are you provokin' a pair a cunts like that?'

Bobby held up his glass, motioning for more vodka, but Timmy shook his head and came around the bar. 'You ain't drinkin' here tonight, Bobby Gold,' he said. 'You're stinkin' . . . and you're lookin' to get yourself jammed up for no good reason that I can see. So be a good guy and fuck off home. Don't you got a cat or somethin' to look after? You ain't doin' nobody any good being here tonight.'

He began wiping down the cable-spool table in front of Bobby with a wet bar-rag. It was the nicest Bobby had ever seen him. Even drunk, he could see that.

See? He did have friends, he thought to himself, as he picked his way to the door. Timmy Moon. Greatest guy on earth. A man who cared. Looking after him like that, making sure no harm came to him. Concerned. Fuck everybody else.

Bobby careened out the door and walked right into Nikki.

'Whoa there, cowboy,' she said. 'I've been looking for you.'

The Apex Coffee Shop was off the lobby of a run-down tourist hotel on 48th street. Bobby drank burnt coffee and tried to focus on the plate of eggs in front of him.

'Eat it,' said Nikki, across from him. 'You'll feel better. Jesus, you were drunk. I've never seen you that way.'

Bobby said nothing, just poked at his eggs with his fork. He hadn't said anything at all since she'd found him, just let her lead him like a trained camel a few blocks away to the overlit coffee shop, watched as she'd ordered for him, sat there until the food arrived, looking at her.

She was in a black leather motorcycle jacket, jeans and a T-shirt, but something was different about her. She was wearing make-up – a little around the eyes, he thought – and was that lipstick? He thought it was.

'I'll wait till you sober up a little before I apologize,' she said, tearing off a piece of toast with short but polished fingernails, the nails cut or chewed in parts, her hands pocked with pink welts.

'I'm okay now,' said Bobby. 'You don't have to apologize. For what?'

'For not making it last night. I'm not like that,' she said, looking away and fumbling for a cigarette. 'I got loaded.' she said. 'Pissed fucking drunk . . . and I fell asleep.'

'It happens,' said Bobby, trying to be noncommittal. 'No big thing.'

'Irregardless . . . It happened to me,' said Nikki, reaching across the table and taking his hand. 'And I'm sorry.' She squeezed his fingers and withdrew her hand awkwardly. 'You know, not for nothin' – but I got all dressed up and everything. I put on a fuckin' dress. Well . . . a skirt anyway . . .'

She laughed suddenly, Bobby smelling vodka on her for the first time, realizing that she too was drunk. 'I even shaved my cat,' she said, an unbecoming half laugh, half derisive snort escaping from her mouth.

'Your what?' said Bobby – picturing his own cat, shorn of hair, trying to imagine her putting up with such a thing.

'My pussy, jerk,' said Nikki, lowering her voice. 'I wasn't kidding before. I was all jazzed up. First date and all. I wanted to make a good impression.'

Bobby didn't know what to say. He stared into his coffee, feeling dizzy, imagining the cleft between her legs devoid of hair, partially shaved, au naturel . . . When she pretended to pick a piece of lint off the sleeve of her jacket, betraying a welcome nervousness he said, 'Fully shaved? Or like . . . only some?' astonished that the question had escaped his lips.

'I left a little bit over the top,' said Nikki, standing up and calling for the check.

'C'mon. I'll show you.'

'Where we going?' he asked, seeing things more clearly, yet somehow even more out of control. 'Where you live?'

'Let's go to your place,' she said, tugging him West. 'You live near here right? The door guy – the big one – said so.'

Making a mental note to fire the loose-lipped doorman, Bobby stopped in his tracks and considered things. No one had ever been inside his apartment. He tried to picture it, as if for the first time, trying to imagine what it would look like to an outsider.

'I need to look at your record collection,' she said, taking his arm in hers and leaning against him. 'I see any Billy fuckin' Joel in there and this ain't gonna happen.'

'Jesus? What you got in here? Fort Knox?' complained Nikki, her hands inside Bobby's jacket as he fumbled with the last lock – a custom-made deadbolt put together for him by an Albanian thief when he'd moved in. The place was clean, he knew. Any guns or cash or 'evidence of wrongdoing' as he'd once heard such things referred to were, as always, securely put away in the concealed floor safe. But Bobby was embarrassed when he flicked on the light. There was something too severe, almost fanatical, about his apartment, he knew. The too-clean, too-polished hardwood floors, the raw brick walls, the always-dusted sound system, the set of free weights neatly arranged in the corner and the heavy bag hanging from the ceiling. His mattress, squared away as usual and tight as a snare drum, rested on a low unfinished wood platform, a copy of *Gray's Anatomy* on the simple, mail-order nightstand. The refrigerator, he knew, was empty save a V-8 and few wedges of leftover pizza in the freezer.

But there was no Billy Joel to be found, he comforted himself. Returning from a long piss in the too-clean bathroom, he found Nikki smiling by his collection of old vinyl, a copy of the first Modern Lovers album in her hand.

'You're an interesting man,' she said, putting the record back in its place, alphabetically between Harold Melvin and Ennio Morricone. She got up, sat down on the bed and began peeling off her clothes, Bobby instinctively looking away for a second before returning his gaze to her sleek, well-muscled back as she bent over to remove her shoes, the crack of her ass, the way her dark hair moved around on her naked shoulders.

'Can you, like, get the light?' she asked, sliding under the covers. 'If you're too drunk to fuck, we can do that tomorrow. Right now, I just want to sleep with you.' She sat upright for a second, an innocuously worried look crossing her face. 'If that's okay?'

Bobby undressed in the bathroom. Took a long shower, washing the stink of Timmy's couch off himself; stood there in the bathroom, forlornly looking at himself in the mirror. He hadn't looked at himself like this in a long time.

When he emerged from the bathroom, in robe and boxer shorts, she was asleep. The cat, who had materialized after no doubt hiding (she'd never seen anyone other than Bobby since he'd taken her in) snoozing by her head. Bobby folded the robe carefully over the single chair, sat for a long time on the edge of the bed, wondering whether to remove the boxer shorts or not, feeling both silly to have put them back on and uncomfortable about taking them off. Finally he whipped them down, pulled up the sheet and got into bed. Nikki didn't move.

In the middle of sleep, he felt fingers on his chest, Nikki's leg working itself between his, her head moving to rest against his shoulder, the absolutely amazing sensation of her breasts brushing against his stomach. His penis immediately stiffened, raising the sheets. He lay there, motionless and afraid, not sure what to do next. A contented noise – it could have been 'Mmmnnn,' came from Nikki's mouth, but that was it. She snuggled a bit closer, then her breathing became more even and she stopped moving entirely. Bobby stared up at complete blackness, tiny flares of color exploding in his head.

'Now that's a penis!' someone was saying. Bobby woke – the room flooded with light from the streakless windows – to see Nikki, resting on one arm next to him, covers pulled down, looking at his cock. He still had a hard-on, a painful one, and he reached instinctively for the covers but she swatted his hand away. She straddled him quickly, leaned forward and kissed him lightly on the lips, then whispered in his ear. 'You're a nice guy, Bobby Gold. Aren't you? That's the big secret isn't it?'

She reached down to grab hold of him, raised herself up for a second, then impaled herself on his erection. The cat woke up, looking alarmed, and fled.

BOBBY AT THE BEACH

Bobby Gold in a black Speedo, his hair still wet from the surf, took a long sip of beer and looked at the pigeons.

'Rats with wings,' he said. 'Beach should be for seagulls. Not pigeons.'

'Lighten up, grouchy,' said Nikki. 'It's a city beach. City beach? City birds.'

'I just don't get why people feed them,' said Bobby, watching an old man in a walker sprinkle breadcrumbs on the boardwalk. 'I mean – it's not like they don't get any food. You ever see a starving pigeon?'

'Cooked a few pigeons in my time,' said Nikki, wiping sweat from between her breasts. She was wearing a tiny little bikini. Color: black – in deference to Bobby, the two of them pale in their dark suits, dark sunglasses and dark hair.

'Yeah? How do they taste?'

'Like chicken.'

The beach was crowded. It was Sunday and barely a foot of sand wasn't occupied with beach chairs, umbrellas, brightly colored blankets, volleyball players, inflatable rafts, body-boards and sunbathers. Bobby and Nikki sat on the edge of the boardwalk, drinking beer from plastic cups and staring out to sea.

'I could live at the beach,' said Nikki. 'If I had enough money? I could definitely live at the beach. Not this beach . . . More like Cape Cod, maybe the Jersey Shore.'

'Maybe. I could see that. Not Florida.'

'No. Definitely not Florida.' Nicole drained the last of her beer, crumpled her cup and hurled it into a trash can a few feet away.

'Nice shot,' said Bobby.

'Three points.'

'Two,' said Bobby.

'I'm thinking of doing something illegal,' said Nikki, apropos of nothing.

'Yeah? Like what?'

'I need money. I want money. I'm thinking about a career change.'

'From saucier to what? Arsonist? Home invader? Bank robber?'

'No . . . I don't know yet. I'm looking for an opportunity. To you know – steal or something. I want to steal a lot of money and then retire to the beach.'

'You don't expect me to—'

'No way! Please . . . I was just sayin''

'And I ain't setting you up with anybody either. What are you fucking thinking? Who put this shit in your head? You been talking to somebody at the Club?'

'No. I just saw a movie on TV last night. Bonnie and Clyde? It looked like fun.'

'You watch the end? They get killed at the end.'

'Not that part. The taking the money part. The driving around real fast in cars part.'

'You'll get grabbed. Believe me. Some knucklehead'll snitch and you'll go to prison. You don't want to go to prison. I'm telling you. You may get plenty of sex there – but the food blows.'

'I know, I know. Don't worry . . . I don't know . . . I just want to do something illegal.'

'You want to do something illegal?' said Bobby, standing up and taking her hand. 'Come with me . . .'

He led her down the wooden ramp to the beach, walking quickly to the right, Nikki hurrying to keep up. It was slightly less crowded at the rear, mostly volleyball players waiting their turn.

'Where we going?' said Nikki.

'Just come on. We're going to do something that's illegal in all 50 states. We're gonna break the law, break the law.'

'Yeah?' said Nikki, interested.

After about four hundred yards, Bobby stopped, looked around, and ducked under the boardwalk, yanking Nikki after him.

'Oh,' she said. 'I think I get it.'

He stuck out a finger and pushed her back onto the cool sand, got down on all fours and pulled off her top.

'People can see us,' she giggled.

'Public lewdness. Indecent exposure,' said Bobby. He peeled

down her bikini bottom, flipped her over and put his tongue up her ass. 'Sodomy,' he added. She jerked like she'd been hooked up to a car battery, moaned and rolled over again, grabbing Bobby's hair to pull his face into her crotch. Bobby's cock protruded almost entirely out of his Speedo. He peeled the Speedo off and lay down next to her.

'I'm gonna get sand in my cunt,' she said, throwing a leg over him and working him inside. 'Go away kid!'

A teenager with a volleyball was standing transfixed, a few yards from the edge of the overhanging boardwalk. He blushed and scampered away.

'Corrupting the morals of a minor,' muttered Bobby, pushing into her as far as he could go.

BOBBY GETS SQUEEZED

Bobby Gold in black Ramones T-shirt, black denims and black Nikes, smeared bone marrow on toast and sprinkled sea salt on it before taking a large bite. His mouth was still full when the man came over and stood by his table, looking at him.

'What the fuck are you eating?'

Bobby raised an eyebrow and finished chewing. The man was tall, about forty-five, with the tired, mean face of an old cop. He wore blue jeans with knife creases, new, white running shoes, and a v-neck T-shirt with a windbreaker over it. His Glock, Bobby guessed, under his left kidney, beneath the T-shirt. There was another gun, something smaller, in an ankle holster on the right. From the man's expression, he did not look like he was going to shoot Bobby – or arrest him. At least not today.

'Bone marrow,' said Bobby, swallowing. 'It's wonderful.'

'Yuk!' said the cop. 'I can't believe you eat that shit.'

Blue Ribbon Bakery on Bedford Street in the Village, was not a place Bobby expected to see cops. Cops ate out in packs, usually at cop-friendly places where raised voices, heavy drinking and the occasional freebie were not unheard of. Blue Ribbon was not like that. This cop had either recognized him from his sheet – or more likely, come looking for him. Bone marrow was a secret pleasure – something Bobby usually indulged in alone. He'd never told Eddie about the place, afraid of being embarrassed, and Nikki couldn't get through a meal without smoking, so he always came here alone. It pissed him off that the cop had clearly decided to brace him here.

'Do I know you?' said Bobby.

'No. I don't think so,' said the man, taking a seat at the corner two-top.

'Have a seat,' said Bobby. 'I guess.'

'Do I look like a cop?'

'Yes. You do,' said Bobby. 'It shows all over.'

'Yeah,' said the cop. 'That's what my wife says.'

'Is there a problem?' asked Bobby. 'I done something wrong?'

'This is a social visit,' said the cop. 'For now, anyway.' He snapped his fingers for a waiter – who was visibly displeased at being summoned in such a fashion – and ordered a coffee.

'Bad Bobby Gold,' said the cop. 'I'm Lieutenant James Connely of the Organized Crime Strike Force. Your name keeps popping up in an investigation we're taking part in and I thought we'd have a chat.'

'Investigating what? I'm a doorman. I work security at NiteKlub. Anything we have to report we report to Mid Town South.'

The cop waved away what Bobby was saying, ignored it completely. 'Please? Okay? We both know the drill, okay? You're nice and polite. You make it look like you're honestly attempting to answer my questions – but you're confused by them because of your immaculate state of innocence. I make some suggestive remarks. Then you simply tell me to fuck off – talk to your lawyer – and how dare you interrupt my bone marrow. Either way you tell me shit and play Dumbo. Okay? Either way you listen. 'Cause you're curious.'

'I'm curious?'

'You should be. Things are happening. Things that are gonna be affecting you and that nice job you have. Or should I say jobs?'

'You gonna tell me what you're talking about? Or we just gonna play I Know More Than I'm Tellin'? You win, by the way.'

'I'm gonna tell you. I'm gonna tell you right now,' said the cop, not acknowledging the arrival of his coffee. He didn't even look at it. 'That little freak you work for? Mr "Eddie Fish"? We're picking up that this goof is gonna get himself greased any minute now. Did you know that? I hear you're close. Like brothers, you so close. Did you know how bad things were?' Bobby just shook his head slowly and kept his mouth shut.

'Eddie is no longer in such good odor with his former associates. People are talking. They're saying Eddie has been unreliable lately. Making a pest of himself. They say that he's popping pills which make him stupid – or should I say more stupid – and some people, apparently have had quite enough. He hasn't been showing up at sit-downs. You know that? They don't like that out there, you know. They really take that the wrong way. They ask a person to come in for a nice talk and he doesn't, they start getting all sorts of ideas. Eddie hasn't been keeping his appointments.'

'Maybe he's been sick. I don't know.'

'He's not sick. Eddie's suckin' that glass dick. He's poppin' a fuckin' drugstore full a goofballs – he's sitting around his fuck-pad on Sutton Place in his undies and ordering take-out. You know that. The man is toast. Tommy V is doing his job for him at the club. Did you know that? Of course not. You wouldn't notice something like a new boss, would you Bobby?'

Bobby just shrugged.

'Shrug all you like. Don't mean shit to me. Alls I'm tellin' you is that your old pal is finished. As soon as he steps out for a sandwich or a blow job, somebody's gonna do him. They got a patch a land-fill all picked out for him. And my question to you is: what do you, Bobby "Gold", nee Goldstein gonna do then? You gonna work for Tommy? You think they gonna let you live?'

'You, they're actually scared of. Eddie's just annoying. What do you think is gonna happen, they drive out Eddie to his final resting place? They gonna let his bestest friend, Big Bad Bobby, live on? Bad Bobby who, they say, did two big bastards up in prison there? The guy they call when somebody needs his bones busted? Eddie Fish's oldest and closest friend and fellow tribe member? You don't think they're worried you might want to do something stupid like take revenge when Eddie goes? You got no job security in what you been doing, Bobby. I can tell you that for free.'

'I can't say I know what you're talking about,' said Bobby.

'I know you can't say,' said the cop, smiling. 'But you know. You know exactly what the fuck I'm talking about.'

The cop took a long sip of his coffee and let out a grateful sigh. 'That's good,' he said. 'That's good coffee.'

'What do you want?'

'Gee. What do you think I want?'

'You want me to snitch. You want me to wear a wire. You want to be my new best pal so you can keep me out of jail, keep me from going to prison. You want to provide me with a new secret identity, large-breasted women, a house in Arizona next to Sammy Bull's. You want me to call you late at night and breathe heavily in to the phone so you can go round up miscreants, arrest people I know. You want me to start giving Tommy V long lingering looks so I can get close to him and then tell you what he dreams about. Forget it. Nobody tells me shit. I don't give a shit about Eddie. And I'm retiring . . .'

'Retiring?' laughed the cop. 'Retiring? What are you gonna do? What can you do – other than bust people up into nice little pieces?'

'I'll find something. I can always work security.'

'What security? Who's gonna hire you? You're an ex-con! You can't get bonded. Nobody who's not mobbed-up is gonna give you a fuckin' job. What are you gonna do? Stand next to an ATM machine the middle of the night? What are you gonna put on the application where it says last place worked? NiteKlub? People gonna say, "Oh, that's the place where that Eddie Fish got killed!" Your boss. Not too good at your job, they might think. Forget

it. You'll be screwed. You'll be dunking fucking fries at Chirpin'
Chicken.'

'I was thinking of going back to school,' said Bobby, telling the
truth for the first time.

'Now that's nice. That might work,' said the cop. 'I saw your old
transcript, you know. You weren't stupid once . . . Had a nice future
up there until you got grabbed driving for Eddie. Eddie skated on
that scot-free didn't he? And what does he do when his old pal,
the guy who went to prison for him gets out? He hires him as a
fucking bouncer. He makes his old buddy into a trained ape. You
could have been, what? A doctor? You were pre-med, right? Things
coulda turned out real different for you, you hadn't started listening
to Eddie.'

'Eddie had nothing to do with it.' said Bobby, irritated. That epi-
sode of his life was a sore point, as Connely clearly was aware.

'Yeah, yeah, yeah, Einstein,' said the cop, 'That's what you said
then. It got you five years. You think your friend Eddie could have
done eight years? He woulda snitched off everybody he ever knew.
He snitched you off, didn't he?'

'Bullshit!'

'Oh yeah? Think? Listen up, moron. Wake up and smell the
coffee. How do you think they picked you up with that carload
a dope, genius? You think they're that smart up there? You just
looked suspicious – so they pulled you over, happened to have a
warrant? Eddie got grabbed two days earlier. He traded the load –
and your ass, for a nice cushy community service, licking envelopes
at some friend of his Daddy's office. His father put it together for
him. You didn't know that?'

'He had nothing to do with it.'

'I got the fucking arrest record. Eddie Fish, detained while enjoying the services of a prostitute and found to be in possession of a controlled substance. You want to see the CI report? The one where he put it all on you? Told the nice troopers what kind of car you'd be driving and where and when? You surround yourself with bad people, Bobby. You're not a good judge of character.'

'Fuck off. This conversation is over,' said Bobby. 'You want to talk more, call my lawyer.'

'Awww . . . Is that any way to be? With an uncertain future in front of you – and a new girlfriend – I thought at least you'd want to listen.'

At the mention of Nikki, Bobby slowly moved his hand across the table and pushed the cup of coffee onto the cop's lap.

'Ooops. Terribly sorry,' said Bobby, without any attempt at conviction in his voice.

Connely stood up and separated the wet fabric of his pants from his crotch, shaking his head.

'That wasn't nice,' he said. 'These are Hagar slacks. Not polyester. All cotton. I'll never get that stain out.'

'I know the feeling,' said Bobby.

It was the people doing the little things around Eddie who saw him at his worst: the drivers, the waiters, bartenders, the doormen who saw him stumble home late, the deli owner at the corner who sold him ice cream when he was too high to talk, the clerk at the video store who rented him pornos. Eddie didn't notice them – so he figured they didn't notice him. They did. The elevator man had seen plenty. Bobby saw that as soon as he stepped inside the gold-and-mirror paneled chamber and told him what floor he wanted. The man rolled his eyes, repeated the floor and pressed the button. Bobby took the ride in silence, still not sure what he was going to do.

The cop had been telling the truth, of course. Bobby could see that now. It's no accident that the rich seemed untouchable. They never hesitate to sacrifice their friends.

The thing to do was to kill him. That's what Eddie would have done, same situation. It's what Tommy V would do – probably what he's going to do, thought Bobby. Right upstairs, charge inside the apartment, pick that treacherous little fuck up by the armpits and throw him off the balcony – 34 floors down. Emotionally, it was the right thing, in that it was the traditional thing to do when betrayed. And intellectually . . . it might be the right thing too. Eddie was a terrible liability right now. Had been for a while. There were plenty of people who would be happy – even grateful – to see him go. The fat men out in Brooklyn would not be unhappy – that's for sure. As a career move it was almost a necessity, the way things were going. Still want that nice job at the club? Want those fat stacks of unaccounted-for bills to keep coming? No problems with the Italian contingent? A life free – or at least free-er – of aggravation? Kill the midget. Hit him once, right on the Adam's apple, pick him up and throw him out the fucking window. Say something Arnold or Clint as he goes down, something like, 'Have a nice flight,' or, 'See you on the street.'

The bell tone rang once when the elevator arrived at Eddie's floor. Bobby looked at the elevator man and mused on whether he would choose to remember him. He glanced at the corner of the ceiling where he knew the camera would be. The window wouldn't do. He heard music from inside the apartment; Curtis Mayfield, 'Little Child Running Wild' . . . knew that Eddie was in a sentimental mood, playing records from the good old/bad old days. Bobby leaned on the bell, heard the music turn off and the shuffle of feet.

Eddie was dressed in a silk bathrobe, no shirt, dress-pants – the bottom half of a charcoal-gray, pinstriped suit. He wore no shoes or socks and he hadn't shaved or bathed in days. Bobby was shocked at how bad he looked – usually, no matter what he was doing, Eddie remembered to get a haircut, have himself shaved if his hands shook. This was not like him. There was a white crust at the corners of his mouth, and the eyes were wild, jangly little pin-pricks surrounded by dark, raccoon-like circles.

'It'sh you,' he said, opening the door and then tottering back to a leather couch. 'Just thinking about you . . . about school.' Bobby looked around the apartment. There were half-empty take-out cartons everywhere: an uneaten brisket sandwich from a deli on top of the wide-screen TV, a half-order of Pad Thai on the cocktail table, bags of Cheetos and chips which had been torn open at the sides, Chinese spread across the floor, a completely melted box of Eskimo pies forgotten in the sink at the bar. Eddie was drinking single malt Scotch and washing it down with Coronas. He must have – at one point – thought about limes. There were two of them on the cocktail table next to the remote control. *The Wizard of Oz* was on the tube, volume down. Eddie turned up the music again: 'Freddie's Dead' this time.

'I hate the flying monkeys,' said Eddie, swatting at something that wasn't there on his face. 'Always hated those fucking monkeys. Remember that time we dropped acid and went to see this?' Bobby remembered. Eddie and he and two girlfriends had gone to see it at the college auditorium, tripping their tits off. One of the girls, Eddie's he thought, had never seen it before. The acid was really starting to kick in when the flying monkeys started getting busy, tearing up the scarecrow and tossing his limbs about, grabbing Dorothy and the dog. The girl couldn't handle it. Started bugging right there. They'd had to leave. Fortunately Eddie had had some thorazines. They'd cooled her right out. Yes, it was Eddie's date, Bobby remembered. He'd gone back to his dorm with the other girl. They'd listened to Roxy Music and John Cale and then she'd given him a memorably dry-mouthed blow job in the small, overheated room. He hadn't been able to come. Hadn't been able to sleep. Just lain there in the dark, the girl's arm across his chest, watching the explosions of color behind his eyes, heart racing.

'What the hell's the matter with you, Eddie?' he said, sitting down across from his old friend. 'Your life looks, like it's turning to shit.'

'It is shit,' said Eddie. 'Fuckin' guineas ruinin' my fuckin' life. Got the IRS crawlin' up my ass, got Tommy's people tryin to put me outta business, the cops with their nose up my ass, and my wife . . . my wife's takin' the kids and the house.'

'Maybe you're taking a few too many pills, Eddie? You thought of that?'

'I know. I know. I need them. I got a preshription. The doctor says I gotta take them.'

'Which doctor?' Eddie always had five or six writing scripts for him at any given moment. His fucking dermatologist wrote him Demarol and Dilaudid and Ritalin and Tranxene. Bobby looked at his friend and boss, sagging into the couch in his bare feet and stained dress-pants, and knew he was looking at a dead man. What could Eddie say now that would make him feel any better? 'I'm sorry?' Seeing Eddie dead would give Bobby no pleasure at all. He could easily just reach over – the state he was now, pinch off his nose with one hand, clamp the other hand on his mouth and watch him go. Eddie was too fucked up, too out of shape to put up much of a struggle.

'This place smells like a Chinese whorehouse,' said Bobby, getting up and sliding open the glass doors to the balcony. 'Jesus! Get some fucking air in here.' He stepped out onto the balcony, looked out across the East River and the Coca Cola sign and Yankee stadium. It was freezing cold, a few snowflakes floated down and then up again with the updraft from the street. Eddie joined him after a few seconds, his robe wrapped tightly around him, his hand gripping fabric under his chin. Eddie collapsed into a chaise longue, spilling his drink.

'I'm fucked,' said Eddie. 'Unless something happens to Tommy, I got no future. You gotta make him go away, Bobby. You gotta do him.'

'I gotta do Tommy Victory, Eddie?' spluttered Bobby. 'You want me to do Tommy? A made fucking guy? What good is that gonna do, Eddie? What the fuck good is that gonna do for anybody?'

'Show them who to respec'' said Eddie, eyes nearly closed. 'Show them who they're fuckin' with . . .'

'That'll work. That'll work great. How long you think they gonna let you live after that? Are you outta your fuckin' mind? You gotta get permission do something like that – and you ain't ever getting permission, Eddie. You even ask, they'll kill you right there. When's the last time those guys ever sided with a Jew over a guinea?'

'Bugsy Seigel,' shouted Eddie. 'Meyer Lansky!'

'Two Jews.'

'Uh . . . give me a minute . . .' mumbled Eddie. 'I'll think of one.'

'It never happened, Eddie. Never. And you ain't no Meyer Lansky. You're a fuckin' stumblebum. You're an unreliable, stuttering, drooling, out-of-control fuck-up with his hand in the fucking cookie jar – and you ain't earning enough – you haven't been earning enough for a while – to make them overlook it any more.'

'Fuck you! What do you know? You don't know me, man . . .'

'I know you, Eddie. I know you in my fucking bones. I known you since I was a skinny kid. I know you for eight fucking years in the jug, smellin' dirty socks and dried jiz and loose farts, you asshole. You sold me out. You fucking dropped a dime on me. And I ain't killing nobody for you no more and I ain't hurtin' nobody no more for you. You can pop your fuckin' pills and drink your fuckin' Coronas and fuck your he-shes and do whatever you want to do 'cause you're not even worth me killing anymore. You're dead already. Worse than dead. Look at yourself!'

Eddie just lay there, staring out into space from under heavy lids. Bobby could hear him breath, a thick, rasping sound. A few seconds later, he was asleep.

Bobby took a yellow cab over to 9th Avenue, the Bellevue Bar at

39th, and found a seat at the end. He should probably call Tommy, arrange a sit-down, work out an arrangement in keeping with the new, inevitable restructing. He should have killed Eddie. Rented a car, taken him out for a drive. Problem over. Anybody still loyal would understand. And Eddie's enemies would appreciate the gesture. But he just didn't have it in him.

There'd be people trying to kill him soon, Bobby understood. If he said nothing. Met with no one. Did nothing. If he just sat here every day, drank himself into insensibility day after day, let them do what they had to do – let the gears turn, the world outside go on without him – sooner or later, someone would come through that door and kill him too.

Nobody at the bar talked to him. When Bobby nodded, the bartender came over and gave him another drink. Soon he was drunk, tapping his fingers to the jukebox. 'Love Comes In Spurts', Richard Hell and the Voidoids. He was deciding whether he wanted to try and live, about what would have to be involved. He'd need a gun. And a car. And money. He had the airweight and the H & K in the floor-safe of his apartment, with a stack of emergency money totalling about 50K. He could get a car no problem. Just a phone call and a taxi to Queens. His Aryan 'brothers' would help – for a while – where the Italians would be unsympathetic. He wouldn't kill Eddie. He wouldn't set him up. But he'd leave him to the wolves this time.

His cell phone rang and he heard objects noisily knocking together on the other end. A second later, 'Pusher Man' off the Curtis Mayfield album was playing over the receiver. Eddie, in a sentimental mood, playing him tunes over the phone. The sound-track to better times.

Bobby's not Here

Bobby Gold nowhere in sight; 5.30 a.m. in the NiteKlub office with Lenny, in ludicrous-looking ski-goggles, working the power saw, Nikki wetting the blade down with water from a kitchen squeeze bottle. Halfway through the second metal pin on the revolving money drop in the safe and Lenny is bathed in sweat, his goggles beginning to steam up.

'Jesus! This thing is taking forever!' says Lenny, turning off the drill for a second and listening for the sound of the floor-waxer. 'You sure that guy's still got his walkman on?'

'He's always got his walkman on,' says Nikki, wiping Lenny's brow with a paper towel, hands – like Lenny's – in surgical gloves from the kitchen. 'C'mon. You're almost through there. Keep at it.'

Lenny turns on the drill and proceeds, bits of metal bouncing off his goggles, stinging his face, lodging in his teeth.

'Ouch!' he complains. 'That hurt!'

'Pussy,' says Nikki.

Finally the sound of the saw changes pitch, the shelf falls free of the last pin. Lenny yanks it out and hurls it into a corner. 'I've gotta piss like a racehorse.'

'Use the trash,' suggests Nikki, pointing at a plastic wastebasket.

While Lenny empties his bladder, Nikki reaches her arm (longer than his) down into the safe and starts pulling out banded stacks of cash. There are a lot more of them than they'd expected.

'Uh . . . Lenny,' she says. 'You see this?'

Lenny, zipping up his fly, turns and looks. The pile of cash on the floor is large – and getting larger. 'Holy . . . shit!'

'No kidding! . . . Holy . . . shit is right!' says Nikki, suddenly damp, a few strands of hair glued to her forehead. 'There wasn't supposed to be that much – was there?'

'Let's get the fuck out of here,' says Lenny.

Lenny leaves first: down the back kitchen stairs, through the service entrance to the hotel. Nikki drops the duffel full of cash out the window and into his arms before following a few moments later. Two hours later, the money divided up and hidden – for the moment under a pile of sweaters in Nikki's closet – the two are sitting in the cellar of Siberia Bar, leaning forward, heads close, talking.

'What's the matter?' asks Lenny, bothered by Nikki's stunned expression, the way she keeps shaking her head.

'I'm alright.'

'No. Really. What's the matter?' he repeats.

Nikki slams back her third vodka shot, her eyes beginning to fill up. 'Everything is different now, isn't it?'

'What do you mean?' says Lenny, playing the tough guy.

'I mean . . . How do we go to work tomorrow? It's gonna be a shit-storm in there. How do I look anybody in the eyes? They'll fucking know.'

'Who are you worried about? The Chef? Ricky? What? Nobody's gonna think it was us! Who would think it was us?'

'There was so much. There wasn't supposed to be that much. I'm worried. I admit it. I'm worried.'

'Fuck them. They're idiots. They'll never find out as long as we don't tell them.'

'I'm worried about Bobby. I don't want him to lose his job.'

'Bobby!? Bobby!! Fuck him! He's not a cook! He's not one of us! What do you care about that asshole?'

'I can't believe this!' shrieks Lenny. His hands trembling, Lenny takes a pull on a beer, missing his mouth and slobbering on his chin. 'You're not going to tell him anything? You're not that stupid.'

'I won't say anything,' says Nikki.

'You better not!' Lenny thinks about this for a while. 'In fact . . . In fact . . . if it looks like he's getting close to figuring anything out – you better tell me. You will tell me, right?'

Nikki waves him away, dismissing the prospect. 'I think you should bug out tonight, Lenny. You can have the money. Okay . . . maybe I'll keep some . . . but you can have most of it. Go to fucking Florida or something. But you should go. That's a lot of money there. You should be fine.'

'What are people gonna say, I disappear the day they find somebody cracked the fucking safe? They'll know!'

'We didn't think this out too good, did we?'

'What do you mean? Stick with the plan. We stick with the plan. That's what we should do!'

'The plan? There was no plan, Lenny. You know what my fucking plan was? You know how stupid I am? My plan was to take the money and get out of the fucking business for a while and maybe rent a nice place somewhere where there's water and maybe a beach and buy some clothes and a TV and like . . . live like a normal person for a while. That was what my plan was, Lenny. You know . . . find a nice boyfriend . . . hole up behind some white picket fucking fence with a garden and like, live like a regular person. You know . . . he goes to like . . . work . . . wherever that is . . . and I putter around the house. I order shit outta catalogs . . . make myself a midday martini . . . watch soap operas . . . cook, like, tuna noodle casserole. Friday nights he comes home, we get dressed up, go out to dinner and maybe a movie – after which we go home and he throws me on a big four-poster bed and fucks me till my nose bleeds.'

'Are you fucking kidding me? Are you nuts? I feel like . . . it's like *Invasion of the Body Snatchers*!! What is with you? My fucking partner is going Suzy Homemaker on me? What the fuck!?'

'I always wanted to putter,' says Nikki, glumly, not looking at Lenny when she says it.

'Putter? You want to putter?'

'You know. Do normal shit. Whatever it is people do. You know. When they're not like us.'

'This is great,' says Lenny, returning from the bar with a Jaeger shot and two beers. 'This is great. I don't even know you anymore.

You couldn't a said this before? You're with the head a fuckin' security . . . you got some weird-ass idea you're gonna turn into some kinda suburban housewife, like in love or some shit. We put down the biggest score of our fucking lives – I'm thinking, buy a couple a kilos a coke and turn that over and, like, open our own place or something—'

'I'm not opening a restaurant with you Lenny, I said that. I always said that.'

'I thought you were kidding. I thought . . . Jesus, Nikki,' says Lenny. 'I thought you liked me. I thought. You know . . .'

Nikki just shakes her head and then leans forward and gives Lenny a sisterly hug. He tries, clumsily to kiss her but she turns her head away, avoiding his mouth.

'I see. I see what it is now,' says Lenny. 'I'm outta here tonight. I'm outta here tonight before you fucking tell the fucking ape-man and blow everything. You . . . you . . . fucking whore!'

Nikki is up in a flash. She reaches back and pops Lenny a good one in the right eye that knocks him back into his seat. Two customers look up quizzically but immediately look away as Nikki glares right back at them and Lenny bursts into tears.

Nikki cradles Lenny in her arms on the hardwood floor of her tiny apartment. They're both still in their coats. Lenny is still crying, his nose running profusely, chest heaving with suppressed sobs. Nikki is petting the back of his head like he's a child, saying, 'That's okay . . . that's okay.' Though, of course, nothing is okay now.

The money has been divided, Nikki keeping only a relatively small share – getaway money should things really turn sour. It's morning already – and Nikki can't remember a time the cheeping birds and early morning garbage trucks have sounded so sinister. Lenny's money is in an airline bag, ready to go.

'You should get out of here,' says Nikki. 'Take your money, get on a train. Go someplace nice and live a little. Get yourself a fucking girlfriend. You're a rich guy, now, Lenny. You'll have to beat them off with a stick.'

'I want you to be my girlfriend,' snivels Lenny, his face collapsing all over again.

'That ain't gonna happen, Lenny,' says Nikki, wiping tears off his receding chin with her sleeve.

Lenny gone, morning commuter traffic in full swing outside her window, Nikki lays on her bed, staring at the ceiling. This was something she never should have become involved in. 'Story of my life, right?' she says out loud.

Her cut, still in the nearly empty duffle bag, sits on the floor – more an affront than a windfall. It isn't the prospect of cops she is worried about. Or the chaos and paranoia and whatever else awaits her when she goes in for work today – if she goes in for work today. It isn't Eddie Fish – who always struck her as a pathetic little shrimp anyway – or what he might do. She could stand up to an interrogation. She'd hide the money somewhere and she'd ride it out. She doesn't feel guilty about taking money from a dishonest shithole like NiteKlub – probably go out of business in a few months anyway (à la carte dinners were getting slower and slower and the party business was drying up for the season). The owners had already skimmed their money out, that was for sure. Only a matter of time till they were all out of work. They deserved it. They'd probably barely notice the money had gone missing. One night's fucking receipts – okay there had been a disconcertingly large amount in there this time – but what would really happen. Now? It isn't getting caught that bothers her. She wasn't going to get caught. It isn't guilt. Or fear – not much anyway. Who'd suspect a chick? Especially now, with Lenny gone? She closes her eyes and tries to forget about the whole thing – pushing the office, the safe, the bag of money on her floor out of her mind. But something keeps intruding. Keeps waking her up, eyes wide open, her breathing getting faster, a painful, swelling ache in her chest.

It's Bobby.

That bothers her. It really does.

Bobby takes it on the Lam

Bobby Gold, in a hastily thrown on black leather jacket, white T-shirt, black denims and sandals, a Heckler and Koch pistol between his legs, stomped on the gas and blew right by a tractor-trailer. 'Roadrunner', the old Modern Lovers tune about cruising Route 128 was on the radio, volume cranked up – appropriate to the circumstances as Bobby and Nikki were on exactly that road, middle of the night, Massachusetts highway, headed for the Cape.

'I forgot to pack a bathing suit,' said Nikki, from the passenger seat. 'Does the music have to be up so loud?'

'Just this song,' shouted Bobby. 'Greatest album ever made. What do you need a bathing suit for? It's winter.'

'The hotel. Maybe the hotel will have a pool.'

'We ain't stayin' in no hotel, baby. Not this trip. People are angry with me. They want to kill me. We stay in a hotel we gotta use a credit card. We use a credit card and it shows up on my statement. Wrong person sees my statement? Bang Bang Dig Dig time.'

'Shit! I thought at least there'd be a pool.'

'You're the one wanted to break the law. You're the one wanted to be an outlaw. Welcome to the wild world of interstate flight.'

Bobby's cell phone rang from inside his jacket. He slowed down slightly, reached, flipped it open and listened. It was Eddie.

'You've killed me,' said Eddie, his voice thick with pills.

'How did I kill you?' said Bobby, annoyed.

'Threw me to the wolves. You left me out on a limb. I've got nobody. I've got nobody anybody's scared of.'

'Buy yourself a pit-bull. Hire a security guard. Do the Witness Protection thing. I don't give a fuck. I'm gone.'

'You're with that bitch?'

Bobby flushed with anger, surprised at the question. 'What the fuck you talking about?'

'That rotten bitch from the kitchen. She busted into the safe last night and took the fucking receipts, Bobby. That's the bitch I'm talking about. She with you?'

'I got to get back to you, Eddie,' said Bobby. 'Call you right back.'

'Uh . . . sweetheart?'

'Yess,' said Nikki.

'Have you been a bad girl? Is there something you're not telling me?'

'Well . . . depends by what you mean by "something" . . .'

'How about this. Did you by any chance take a SawZall and break into the club's safe last night?'

Nikki said nothing for a while as she considered her answer. A 16-wheeler blew by them on the highway followed by silence.

'I might have done something like that. I'm very mechanically inclined. My brother works in a machine shop.'

'That's nice. That's very nice. And last night, when you and whoever helped you in this boneheaded fucking venture were taking stacks of money out of the safe. Did it occur to you, perhaps, whose money exactly it was you were absconding with?'

'Well . . . I guess we figured it was Eddie's.'

'And who does Eddie owe money to do you think? Who do you think Eddie's partners are?'

'Some German asshole. I've seen him. He's always trying to fuck the waitresses.'

'That's what we call in the business, the "straw owner" cupcakes . . . That's what they call on television cop shows, "the front man".'

'Uh-oh,' said Nicole. 'You're about to tell me whose money it really was, aren't you?'

'Yes. Yes I am,' said Bobby.

A little while later they were crossing the Buzzard's Bay Bridge onto the Cape and Route 6. Bobby's phone went off again and he rolled down the window on the driver's side, hurled it out over the rail into blackness.

'Your phone's ringing,' said Nikki.

'I know,' said Bobby.

'This guy you mentioned is not a very nice man, I take it?' said Nikki.

'You could say that,' said Bobby.

'I got nineteen thousand dollars,' said Nikki. 'Would he like, hunt us down and kill me for that?'

Bobby did a little quick math in his head, abandoning his equations after a few seconds.

'Well . . . let's just say he's not exactly going to be looking for his money back. It'll cost him half the nineteen by the time he finds us. Thing is, with Tommy, guys like Tommy? It's the principle of the thing, you see. That's the problem.'

'So, I kind of got us in trouble, didn't I. And we were already in trouble.'

'I was in trouble. Before? Before you could have dodged out anytime you got tired of chowder and grinders and cold nights. Now you got a problem too.'

'Bummer.'

'Will they know where to look?'

'Eddie'll know – eventually. Me and him used to come out here summers for a while.'

'Will he tell Tommy?'

'That's the question, isn't it?'

'Suddenly, Provincetown doesn't seem far enough away.'

'No, it doesn't, does it?'

'I was in it with a friend. You think—' Bobby didn't let her finish her sentence.

'I think they got your friend hooked up to a car battery by now. I bet he's coughing up whatever his cut was and whatever he knows or suspects or can dream up. I think when they're done asking him questions they're going to drive him out to Jersey and dig a hole and put him in it. Maybe they'll shoot him first.'

'Oh,' said Nikki. 'Oh.'

She sat quietly in the dark for a while. Bobby thought he could hear an occasional sniffle between cigarettes. He kept his eyes on the road, speed just under the limit, thinking about what to do next. A place in town was now out of the question. He knew somebody who could hook them up with a dune shack which would have to do until they figured out what to do next. Terrible things were going to happen in New York. People were going to die. Eddie being 'boy most likely to'. He figured he'd wait. See who fell and who survived before he made any rash moves. With luck, something bad could happen to Tommy in the shake-out to come. Letting some girl sauté cook take his crew off for a night's receipts didn't look good. Such things were bad for you, the business Tommy was in. With any luck, a few whispers, some young Turk would maybe make the problem go away. Maybe Eddie would turn State's evidence, go off to Arizona and rehab, keep Tommy and his people hunkered down filing motions and answering summons. On the other hand, maybe Tommy would come after them with everything. Maybe Tommy would go have a nice talk with Paul and tell him what a terrible thing that Eddie's man Bobby did – how he cast aspersions on Paulie's sainted, no-doubt-virginal daughter to get out of a previous jam, how he was a thieving, cowardly, and potentially dangerous problem who had to be taken care of immediately – along with his puttana. This, of course, was the more likely scenario.

*   *   *

After a month, when nobody came, when no strangers had been noticed in off-season Provincetown, where people tended to notice such things, they began to visit town more often, usually for breakfast at the Tip for Tops'n on Bradford Street, or for dinner at a Portugese fisherman's joint where Nikki liked the squid stew. Nikki took a job part-time at a pizzeria, spinning pies and Bobby did a little roofing and carpentry, a little day labor at the boatyard. It was cold and crisp during the day, but with brilliant, sharp-focussed light, the sunsets spectacular, and the sound of foghorns and boat whistles, the smells of fish and salt spray, the slowed down, more relaxed life of an off-season resort town making Cape Cod seem much farther away from whatever was happening in New York.

Bobby read the *Times*, religiously, looking for news of dead organized crime associates, and Nikki read *Vogue* and *Marie Claire* and *Bazaar* and planned her wardrobe for the spending spree they were going to have whenever they made their next move. Whatever that was. At night it was freezing cold in their beach shack – and on really cold nights, they'd leave the oven on with the door open and huddle naked under four or five blankets, noses cold, giggling, and without care. Bobby kept the H&K under the pillow for the first few weeks then moved it to the night table. They fucked almost every day and spent hours just staring wordlessly down at the sea. They shot pool at the Governor Bradford, bought a cheap TV set from a Portugese fisherman and watched snowy, blurry reruns of old sitcoms under the covers, Bobby getting out in the cold to move a clothes hanger/antennae around the room from time to time – for better reception. Nikki cooked now and again – usually something simple, but occasionally a classic French feast, serving *paté de canard* and salmon with sorrel sauce on paper plates, washed down with fine wine in plastic cups. Bobby never asked her about the stolen money or why she should have done something so stupid and suicidal. It was assumed that at some point they'd really run away. Bobby favored the far East. Nikki was partial to the Caribbean or Mexico.

Nineteen grand, Bobby might have pointed out, was not going to be enough for both of them.

In April, Eddie Fish made the papers. A full-cover shot in the *New York Post*, Eddie interrupted at dinner, a mouthful of veal chop with the sauce from the chicken, laid out on the cold tile floor, shirt pulled up, head leaking black onto white, dead as dead could be. His eyes were half open and there was food on his shirt.

'I think I need more guns,' thought Bobby, heading back to the dune shack. 'I really do.'

But when he got back Nikki was asleep, dozing really, mid-afternoon, one arm thrown over her eyes, mouth slightly open, blankets just below her breasts. Bobby quietly got undressed and slipped under the covers with her. She curled into a ball and worked her way dreamily under his arms, seeking warmth. He felt her slowly unravel, throwing a leg over his, then a hand around his back, the other one seeking something, finding it. Her head disappearing completely under the covers.

*   *   *

When he woke up it was dark and he couldn't hear the generator. The window by the bed flew off its hinges, blew apart, glass suddenly in his hair. It took a second to realize that people were shooting at them; window, door, through the walls, the reports of three, maybe four weapons muffled by the sand, whipped away in the wind.

It's always the little things you remember when terrible things happen.

Bobby would remember the splinter he got when he jumped out of bed, his bare feet scrambling for purchase on the floor. He would remember the way his fingers felt useless and rubbery as he tore open the drawer and grabbed for the H&K. He would always remember the sound Nikki made when he shoved her out of bed onto the floor – and that his cock stuck to his leg for a second as he ran for the door firing.

He'd remember that the first man he saw was wearing a shooter's vest and earmuffs and that when Nikki was hit she made an 'Ouch!' noise like she'd just cut herself on a grapefruit knife.

Niteklub gone. Family . . . long long gone. And Nikki? Not here. That was for sure. He missed everything about her. Her hair. Her sardonic smile. The not knowing what was going to come out of her mouth next. Her scent. Recalling it made his chest hurt.

He was the driver now. No longer a passenger in a tightly circling cab. And he had seen the world – the Eastern part of it anyway: Bora Bora, Singapore, Japan, China, Vietnam, Laos, Thailand, Cambodia, a blurry film strip of temples, *wats* and mini-bars, transit lounges, buffet breakfasts, noodle shops, maimed beggars, stone-faced soldiers, brown-skinned children in mud and rags calling 'hello!' 'bye-bye!' from riverbanks and stilt-supported houses. He'd seen moon-faced whores and eager cyclo-drivers, smoked opium in a tin-roofed shack under a driving rain, stayed in cheap neon-lit hotel rooms: bed, fan, TV set showing only Thai kick-boxing and MTV Asia, 'karaoke-massage' in the lobby and someone else's hair on the complimentary plastic comb and everywhere the smell of wood smoke, the overripe camembert odor of durian fruit, fish sauce, chicken shit and fear. The soundtrack to the new not-so-improved Bobby Gold Story was the sound of a million throbbing generators, the endless droning of yet another pressurized cabin, the whoosh of turbines, the low-throated gurgle of turbo-props, the admonitions in pidgeon English, Thai, Khmer, Vietnamese and Chinese that one's seat cushion could be used 'as a flotation device' and to refrain from using cell phones or electronic devices.

He'd bought a gun in Battambang – an old Makarov pistol with extra shells. Partly for self-protection, as what constituted a crime in these parts depended largely on how much money one had in one's wallet and who one's cousins were. But also with the half-formed idea that one of these days he might want to put the gun in his mouth and pull the trigger. It seemed a romantic place to die, Siem Reap, in the shadows of Angkor Wat and Angkor Thom – to be found dead under the big stone heads at Bayon; the reports, if any, of his demise to read something like, 'found dead of a gunshot wound in Siem Reap'. It just as well might read Battambang, or Pailin, or Vung Tau or Can Tho or Bangkok. It made little difference, as there was, really, no one left back home to read or care or be impressed by such a romantic demise.

'Oh yeah, the dude with the ponytail? The guy who used to work security? He was fucking the sauté bitch, right?' was what they'd say in the kitchen

'He was doing Nikki, right? What ever happened to her, man? She was good on the line,' was what they'd say. Then someone would notice a song they didn't like on the radio and go to change the station and then they'd talk about something else.

It was a very nice hotel – though an empty one. Black-and-white tiled floors, ochre colored walls with mahogany and teak moldings. The ceiling of the bar was decorated with finely drawn murals of elephants and Khmer kings and the agreeable waiters wore green and white sarongs and knew to a man how to make a proper Singapore Sling or a dry martini or vermouth cassis.

Bobby was well-liked at the hotel as he was neither Russian nor German and didn't insist on bringing whores to his room like the other guests. He spent his days at the temples or at the riverbank and his evenings at the bar slogging through Malreaux and Greene and Maugham and Tim Page, trying to absorb their enthusiasms. Their lives so different than his own. 'I love you,' she'd said and squeezed him tightly, her fingers sinking into his back. He'd kissed her and tasted blood and then she'd slipped – as Jim Morrison once put it – 'into unconsciousness'.

He'd been drinking too much . . . and smoking bad weed – the rough-tasting Khmer smoke that cost only a stack of worthless riels per kilo and the anti-malarial pills he'd been taking once a week were putting the screws to his head, giving him nightmares. He'd wake up, middle of the night with his chest pounding after a particularly violent dream, smelling blood, his arms actually aching from fighting off full-color phantasms.

Here's one dream Bobby had:

Bobby Gold at eight years old, in blue jeans, high-top sneakers and pale blue T-shirt standing in the schoolyard, a ring of faceless children around him in a tightening circle. It was dodge ball they were playing – and Bobby was it – the bigger kids, pale and dead-eyed, aiming the big rubber ball at his face. Suddenly the action switched and it was Eddie Fish standing in the perfectly round gauntlet, Bobby holding back the ball, taking aim, throwing it. Eddie cowering, the ball (Bobby could smell the rubber, read the manufacturer's name: 'VOIT') striking Eddie flush on the nose, smashing it flat, the blood coming, coming, not stopping, as Eddie, in shorts, screaming silently and Bobby's head filling with the smell of rust, of school erasers, Juicyfruit, disinfectant, latex paint, the taste of chewed pencils. The others come at Eddie with garden hoes now, striking first the hard schoolyard asphalt, then flesh, Bobby hearing the sound as metal buried itself in bone, felt the vibrations in his spine with each solid whack.

He woke up in cold, wet sheets, gasping, then smoked a half a pack of 555s, afraid to go back to sleep.

An ancient Antonov to Phnom Penh, seats broken, seatbelt useless at his side, the cabin filled with steam a few minutes after take-off – the other passengers actually laughing when the stewardesses handed out the in-flight meal, a plastic-wrapped sandwich and a roll in a cradboard box – wings yawing dangerously as the plane touched down. Overnight in Bangkok in a gigantic airport hotel, a twenty-minute walk to his room from the lobby, a Philippine trio singing 'Rock The Boat' in the lounge, Tiger beer in the mini bar. Transfer at Narita. A packed flight – tourist class – to LAX, taxi to a Japanese-owned hotel in West Hollywood.

The cocktail lounge was filled with well-dressed people talking on cell phones in amber-colored light. The women were well made-up, hair done, heels, the men in jackets with recently polished shoes. They sat in plush, upholstered chairs and overstuffed couches, drinking novelty drinks off tiny little tables. British techno-soundtrack music issued from hidden speakers. A waiter offered Bobby a complimentary spring roll from a tray. He'd never felt so detached from his own country. It smelled of nothing here, only air-conditioning, the figures around him in the lounge moving dreamlike through space like characters in a film. A woman at the next grouping of chairs looked at Bobby then whispered something to her date – he turned around for a second, glanced at him, then snapped his head away as if frightened. Bobby sat there like a stone obelisk, his ice melting in his drink, horrified. There was something indecent in all this affluence. He'd just come from a place where everything smelled, where children tugged your sleeve and begged for your leftovers, where amputees slithered legless across the street and the police felt free to open fire at any time. He felt like he was on another planet, the languid movements of the young, graceful crowd somehow a cruel and terrible affront to the way he knew the world to really be. Bobby thought, 'I could kill anyone in this room and never feel a moment's guilt.'

He was coming apart here. He had to get out.

He rented a Ford Focus through the desk, set out for Arizona in the morning.

He'd never seen America but he saw it now. Out the window, one strip-mall led to another, then desert, then more strip-mall, filling stations, fast-food joints, car dealerships, desert again. The kids were fatter than in Asia; baggy pants, caps on backwards, fierce acne, sullen looks as they watched him pump self-serve gas, grab a bite. He was old, he realized, nothing to say to anyone anymore – if he'd ever had anything to say, America suddenly a vast ocean of blonde hair, crenulated thighs, fanny packs and Big Gulps. He aimed the car at the horizon and drove, a six pack of Budweiser in a styrofoam cooler on the seat next to him, a gas station map his only guide. He bought new clothes at a mall in Tucson; khaki pants, a denim shirt, aviator glasses, a pair of shoes which the clerk assured him would 'last a life-time', changed at a Motel 6 after a swim in a pool that stank of chlorine. He arrived in the small development community at dusk; cookie-cutter houses, ranch-style with little signs announcing family names over identical mailboxes, driveways filled with SUVs, muscle cars, children's toys. Just outside of town was a mega-mall with food court, deca-plex cinema, a chain hotel with heated pool and 'convention facilities'. The 'old' part of town dated back only to the forties; similarly identical homes – built like the newer ones all at once – these to accommodate the wartime aviation and munitions industry who'd once had factories in the nearby desert. And a single strip of shabby businesses; superette, hardware store, a movie theater turned furniture outlet, city hall, police department, bowling alley, a few shops selling nostrums and notions.

She worked at Duke's Pizza, spinning pies in the front window. She had her hair tied back with a red kerchief – to keep it from burning in the oven, and she wore a tight white T-shirt that revealed a slight impression of nipple, a long, sauce-stained apron. From across the street, he couldn't see where the bullet had entered. She was spinning pie now, two fists working the dough ever larger, a twirl with the fingertips of the right hand, and then the pie disappeared up and out of frame, reappearing a second later. Nikki looked grimly satisfied as she slung the floppy, white object back and forth between her wrists. A single strand of hair worked loose from the headband hung over her face, giving her an appearance of heartbreaking earnestness. Below the window frame, she ladled sauce, sprinkled cheese, then moved the finished pizza on a long wooden paddle into the back of a deck oven, yanked it free with a hard, unhesitating jerk of the arm, muscles flexing.

He rolled up his window, ducking back as she pushed away the strand of hair from her face, blew out, stared out the window at the empty street, squinting in the mid-afternoon glare.

Nikki in hiding. New name. New address. She'd snitched him off – as arranged bedside at the hospital – in return for protection. He looked up and down the street and saw no one who looked like a cop or a fed or a US Marshal. As arranged, she'd sent him a single postcard, care of a rooming-house in Goa, telling him where she was and that she was okay.

She'd had nothing to say – no 'direct knowledge' as lawyers like to phrase it – about Tommy Victory. Bobby had been all she'd had to offer and he'd insisted. She'd needed something to pay the toll – and an organized crime 'associate' with multiple bodies on his resumé had seemed like an easy out. She'd been in the hospital for three months – and physical therapy for a year after that. He'd had to do something.

'Why?' she'd asked him. 'Why does it have to be you?'

'Because it's all we've got,' he'd said. 'Because they might come back. Because what Tommy's people want from you is too high a price for anyone to pay.' The person they'd send, if they could find her would have been someone just like he had once been. A professional. Someone who knew how to hurt people, how to ask hard questions. Someone who didn't flinch when people screamed. Someone for whom another life extinguished was just another day at work.

Because Tommy knew that Bobby was out there somewhere. Because he knew what he was likely to do.

Bobby left town quietly, saying nothing. He didn't call her at the shop. He didn't even wave.

He dropped the car in Tucson, rented another – under yet another name – and made the long, long drive cross country, New York finally appearing beyond the George Washington Bridge. He bought a banged up .38 Airweight from a Serbian safecracker he'd known upstate and checked into a no-tell motel just across the river in Fort Lee.

Tommy Victory, in a smart tweed jacket, brown turtleneck and pleated slacks, approached his Lincoln town car in the cool autumn Connecticut dusk. A dead leaf stuck to his loafer, and he stopped to peel it off distastefully with a fingertip before standing by the rear passenger door of the idling car. He knocked on the smoked glass window for his chauffeur/bodyguard, and when no response came, opened the door, irritated, and heaved himself inside, mouth already open to chew out his sleeping driver.

He wasn't sleeping. Tommy could see that right away. His head lay on the seat back at an unnatural angle, the neck broken. The door on the far side suddenly opened and Bobby Gold, looking thinner and tanner than he'd remembered him, was sitting next to him, grabbing him by the hair and pulling his head back. The .38 broke a tooth as it went in Tommy's mouth. Tommy's last thought was of bridgework as he heard the words, 'Hello, Tommy,' matter-of factly spoken as Bobby pulled the trigger, pushed the barrel ever deeper down Tommy's throat.

Bobby emptied the gun, the car filling with cordite smell, the report deafening in the enclosed space. When Tommy sagged back onto new leather, a single perfect smoke-ring issued from his open mouth.

Bobby Gold, in a purple and blue sarong, feet bare, drank Tiger beer and watched children washing their hair in dark, brown, muddy water at the riverbank. A water buffalo strained to pull a plow with a missing wheel in a rice paddy in the distance. A khmer in a khaki shirt and shorts, a red krama covering his head from the sun, collected sticks from the roadside. Bobby brushed a persistent fly away from the corner of his mouth and lit another 555, sat there smoking, yearning for pizza.